GIRL ON THE HEIGHTS

As the star singer at 'The Purple Pelican' nightclub Janie Smith was fast making a name for herself and her sordid slum upbringing slipped further into the past. Then her step-sister Celia came back into her life. She wanted to be in show business, but she had little talent and had no intention of working to improve it. Roger Phillips, Janie's accompanist, loved her and could see that Celia was ruining Janie's career. When Celia went to a rival agent Roger was prepared for a showdown. But not the sort that took place. Celia was found strangled—in Janie's house.

GIRL ON THE HEIGHTS

GLADYS GREENAWAY

LYTHWAY PRESS
BATH

First published 1968
by
Hurst & Blackett Ltd
This Large Print edition published by
Lythway Press Ltd
Bath
by arrangement with the copyright holder
1980

ISBN 0 85046 872 8

British Library Cataloguing in Publication Data

Greenaway, Gladys
    Girl on the heights. – Large print ed.
    I. Title
    823'.9'1F   PR6057.R3/

    ISBN 0–85046–872–8

Photoset, printed and bound
in Great Britain by
REDWOOD BURN LIMITED
Trowbridge & Esher

GIRL ON THE HEIGHTS

CHAPTER ONE

The Purple Pelican was a nightclub where men could take their wives and on Saturday nights it was usually full. The décor was restful, the service good and the food excellent. Waiters moved swiftly and efficiently between the tables, the atmosphere was gay and it was expensive. A place to dine well and be entertained discreetly.

The lights dimmed and there was a sudden hush. A spotlight shone on the curtains at the back of a small stage. As they parted a tall, slim girl came through. Janie Smith was wearing a long, silver gown, high at the throat with long, tight-fitting sleeves, her thick, fair hair fell loosely round her face. She wasn't beautiful by any means but there was a simplicity about her that drew your attention. As she came forward there was a trickle of notes from the piano and her voice joined them, richly, gently, with no effort.

'Midnight girl, sleeping all the day, waiting till the moon sheds her silver ray.'

Trite words but there was a moonlight quality about the singer which lifted the song out of the mundane. She came down from the stage and strolled between the tables, pausing

1

here and there to smile into the eyes of a patron, man or woman. Friendly but no more.

The song over she went back to the piano where Roger's strong fingers ran over the keyboard as if he wasn't caring about the notes. Actually he was listening for every tiny inflection in her voice, following with the aptitude of the born accompanist. She leant against the piano, finished the last line of 'Midnight Girl' and then spread her arms wide as if to embrace the whole of her audience. When the applause died down she went over to a tall stool for her next number. An 'oldie' from the thirties, especially for the older patrons. Her easy smile, her warm voice, the utter simplicity of her approach and the complete difference from 'pop' had given her a name.

A certain amount of luck, a great deal of hard work, enough good looks to interest the men without annoying the women and a lot of cockney good sense had carried her well up the ladder. She could get to the top, Janie knew that without a doubt, but she wasn't sure yet if she wanted to. The higher you climb the farther you fall and Janie, for all her pluck, was scared of falling. And just now she was going through a bad patch.

What was Celia doing?

The number was as simple as breathing. The words and notes flowed automatically. She perched on the stool and drew her slim legs up so the heels of her shoes hooked over the rung and she was back in Lilac Grove, sitting on the topmost step of the broken-down terraced house with the blank factory wall opposite. The shouts and screams of the playing children, the distant noise of the traffic in the High Street were all there. God, how she had hated it! The filth, the rows, the untidy, dirty rooms and her stepfather, Tom Craddock. Without him she might not have hated it so much but he was the focal point. In those days she could not have put her thoughts into words, she felt a deep contempt with a certain pity for her slovenly, inadequate mother but for Tom Craddock there was a sickening hatred.

She bowed her way from the stage and went to her dressing room. Roger followed.

'What's the matter, Janie? You weren't at your best.'

She looked at Roger, startled out of her carefully built self-assurance. Was she allowing herself to slip?

'What are you talking about? The audience liked me.'

'Because they don't know you as well as I do but if you let your mind wander as it did tonight they will soon realise you are not completely with them. What's wrong, Janie?'

'These damn contact lenses were irritating. They're new ones.' She slipped them out expertly and bathed her eyes.

'You're not a very good liar. It isn't the contact lenses. It's Celia, isn't it?' She went on bathing her eyes. 'You're a fool, Janie. She's not only bad, she's dynamite and while you have her with you you are waiting for the explosion. If you are not careful she will not only mess up your life but your career.'

Janie put the contact lenses back and lit a cigarette. 'She is my sister, a fact that you seem to forget.'

'I don't get the chance. You rub it in too often. If you are fool enough to spend your hard-earned money on that good-for-nothing family of yours that's up to you but there is no need to let them, or rather Celia, muck up your career. She may be your sister but she's a lazy slut and not to be trusted.'

She didn't bother to deny it. Roger had eyes in his head and they spent a good many hours practising at her house at Hampstead. Celia getting up at midday when she was supposed to be at secretarial college. Janie wondered how many times she had attended. Not many, that was for sure. Until this morning she had kept up a pretence of going. She had

4

no class in the morning or not before eleven! There were days when she had already gone out when Janie came down but that was seldom before ten-thirty. When she was there arguments were continual and Janie found it more and more difficult to hold on to her temper. This morning things had really come to a head. Celia had wandered into the studio wearing a grubby nylon housecoat over a flimsy nightdress and with last night's make-up still round her blue, blue eyes. Flinging herself down on the settee she stared at them with amusement which was as old as Lilith. At seventeen Celia was not only beautiful but old.

'You should be at school, Celia.' Janie was angry although she knew it was futile. Celia had made herself one of the household and she didn't care a button what Janie wanted.

'Don't talk crap! On a Saturday morning! Not that I intend to go there to please you.' She was so complacent. 'What the hell do you think I am? Go to that bloody secretarial college and end up as a bloody typist earning ten pounds a week. What do you take me for? There's more money to be made in your game and if you can do it why shouldn't I?'

'Because you are not prepared to work as your sister does even if you had her talent, which you haven't.' Roger had looked at her

5

with angry brown eyes.

'You mind your own bloody business. Work! I bet she wouldn't have got anywhere without Mr. High-and-mighty Banstead and how did she manage to get him interested I'd like to know? You're a sucker, Roger Phillips, but I'm not. Put that up your jumper or down your trousers along with anything else you have there—if you have anything, which is doubtful!'

Roger's sallow skin flushed with embarrassment and he glanced at Janie uncomfortably. Janie's green eyes glittered and her hands clenched and unclenched but it was the cold fury in her voice that startled him even more than Celia's vulgarity.

'Get out of here, you filthy little guttersnipe, and go to your room. I'll talk to you later. Don't you dare to come in here again.'

Celia got up from the settee and walked to the door with hips swinging. There she turned and made a suggestive gesture and, childishly, stuck out her tongue, but for all the childishness the large blue eyes were full of malice. Roger felt sick. Janie stood quite still, her face stony, her hands tightly clenched but her breast rose and fell as if she no longer had control of her breathing. After a few moments she walked to the cocktail cabinet and, pouring herself a glass of water,

6

drank it as if she was parched and then lit a cigarette.

'I can't work any more today, Roger, but don't worry, I'll be all right tonight but I won't use that new number. I'll do "Midnight Girl", instead.'

The memory was still with her, her stomach revolted at it. She looked up at Roger and blinked, then gave him a sudden, urchin grin.

'All right, she's a slut but she hasn't had much chance to be anything else and I want to give her the chance. She's the only one in the family who shows any promise and if I left her with the rest of them she would do the same as Angela. Get into trouble with the first man that comes along and then marry him if he'd marry her or leave the baby to be dragged up by my mother and go on working in a factory where her mind and language would get even worse than it is now.' She shrugged her thin shoulders. 'After all, she's only been with me three months but I wish to goodness her vocabulary would improve. The only adjective she seems to know is bloody. But what is three months against seventeen years? Give her time. She was a sweet little kid and very fond of me.'

'Monkey face, I hate to say this to you but you are wrong. I doubt if Celia has ever been

7

fond of anyone but herself. She's the sort to use people and she's using you and instead of being grateful for what you are trying to do for her she is consumed with jealousy. Instead of seeing that you have got where you are by hard work and talent she wants it the easy way. Don't look so hurt. Face up to facts. Come along, you look dead beat. I'll drive you home. I don't need my car tonight. I can walk to my flat without undue strain.'

His grin was infectious and she smiled back at him. If only she didn't feel sure he was right.

'Come in and have a cuppa with me before you go home, Roger. I know I'm tired but I can't sleep yet. I'm handling Celia badly and I know it. You saw the way I lost my temper today and it's getting worse. The slightest thing and I blow my top.'

'Glory hallelujah! I marvel you don't turn the little blighter out!'

'Because you've never lived in Lilac Grove. It's over ten years since I left but I know what it can do to you.'

They went into the neat, modern kitchen. So often they drank a cup of tea there after the show but tonight it wasn't the same. There was an empty glass and a plate holding the remains of a meal on the table. An empty can on the draining board, a soup plate and saucepan in the sink. Crumbs on the floor, cigarette ends on the plate and ash everywhere. Jane looked at it distastefully.

'Shades of Lilac Grove. There were always cigarette ends on plates or on the floor. I've a feeling my mother didn't know there were such things as ashtrays.'

She filled the electric kettle and switched it on and then cleared up the mess.

'Roger, do you think if I encouraged Celia to sing it might help?'

'No!'

'I begin to think I should have encouraged her rather than stopped her. There's lots of youngsters with little or no talent who go places.'

'I know but they've got something she hasn't got. A certain warmth. She's got looks, a voice like an alley cat and precious little more unless it is envy.' Janie knew that wasn't the real reason he didn't want Celia to sing. She was cheap and vulgar and he didn't want anyone to hear her and know they were sisters. 'Janie, stop imagining that what you have done she may be able to do. If she could she'd have got out like you did. You had no more chances but look what you have made of yourself.'

'You're wrong. I've had a lot of help from a lot of people, including you. The best chance

9

of the lot was being a little bastard and never being allowed to forget it.' There was an unexpected amusement in her voice. 'It set me apart from the rest of the family. Made me feel different.'

'Good God, I should have thought that made it much worse.'

'No, it got me away from there at fourteen. Tomorrow I'll talk to Celia. In the meantime I'll put her out of my mind. Now let's talk about the new number. Do you think it would be better at the piano or walking?'

The subject of Celia was dismissed and by the time they had drunk their tea Janie looked more like her usual self. She saw Roger to the door, closed it gently after him and went upstairs. Before she reached the landing she heard Celia's door close. So, she had been listening again. Dear God, what a fool she was making of herself because Celia had come to her with tear-wet eyes and told her she couldn't stay at home any longer. Was the story that she was afraid of her father true or just a means of getting her sympathy and into her life? She knew Tom Craddock could be violent, she had felt his hand on her cheek a good many times and his belt on her back at others but she had never seen him brutal with his own children. That had set her apart but it wasn't his violence that had

10

taken her away from Lilac Grove.

She went into the bathroom and turned on the taps. Fanny slept on the top floor and nothing would disturb her and Celia was awake. She lay in the hot water longer than she intended and tried to get her thoughts in order. It was a long time since she had let the past interfere with the present but tonight she could think of nothing else. If she hadn't heard Celia's door close she might have managed to keep it at bay but now it was with her as if it was more important that the present.

Why had Tom Craddock married her mother? Why had her mother married him? She tried to picture her mother in her late teens and early twenties. Probably as lovely as Celia, a perfect blonde with eyes as blue as a summer sky and a figure that turned the heads of most men. Her own figure was far too thin and without a good hairdresser her hair was mousy.

She didn't know how old she was when her mother married Craddock, she didn't know who her father was. Sometimes she wondered if her mother did! She didn't remember when Angela was born for she was barely two at the time. Then there was Tommy. She remembered that clearly. She had sat on the dirty stairs with Angela by her side listening to her

11

mother's groans and been terrified. Then there had been Margaret followed by Celia and then young Gary. All of them crowded into three dirty rooms with Tom Craddock coming home drunk whenever he had any money and her mother getting more and more slovenly and less and less inclined to do anything. Meals of bread and margarine, fish and chips or faggots. If Tom Craddock had not perpetually informed her that she was not his kid but a little bastard and God alone knew who her father was she might have accepted things but she didn't know who her father was. It was a compensation. He could have been anyone. He could have been someone important. School books filled her head with dreams and, being near-sighted, she wasn't interested in playing games with the other children. She pictured her father, tall, handsome, perhaps a bit like Dr. Herbert who came when Margaret was ill. Margaret had been crying with pain on the frowsy bed in which the four girls slept and Janie was in the kitchen with Gary in her arms. Dr. Herbert came into the kitchen to wash his hands. He had given the dirty towel a look and then taken a clean handkerchief from his breast pocket and wiped his hands on that and suddenly turned to her and smiled.

'Are you the eldest?' She nodded. Her eyeglasses had slipped down her nose and gave her an old-fashioned air. 'Your mother is lucky to have such a little woman to mind the baby!' He pushed the wet handkerchief into his pocket and Janie wished the towel hadn't been so dirty. 'How many of you are there?'

'Angela, Tommy, Margaret, Celia and Gary.'

'What's your name?'

'Gloria.' His hair was silvery and his face kind. A nice man for a father.

'Well, Gloria, your sister has appendicitis and I am going to call an ambulance. When will your father be home?'

'He ain't my father and I don't know.'

'I thought . . .'

She didn't wait for him to finish, just shrugged her shoulders. 'I'm not one of 'is. I'm the bastard.'

'Really!' He gave her an understanding look. 'That makes you rather different, doesn't it?'

Being the butt of Tom Craddock's temper never mattered quite so much after that. If he walloped her she thought that if she could find her father her life would alter. She didn't know how she was going to do it but she took to wandering after school, watching people, picking out the sort of house she would like

13

to live in, getting her ears boxed when she came home late but not caring.

In Lilac Grove and the district surrounding it kids grew up fast. They didn't believe in Santa Claus nor that babies were brought by the doctor or found under gooseberry bushes. They knew the facts of life from an astonishingly early age. Gloria (that was long before she became Janie) would listen to the grunts and struggles and the creaking of the bed that her mother and stepfather shared and hope to goodness there wouldn't be another baby. There was no repugnance, just an acceptance of life as she knew it. The cool indifference of childish knowledge. She went on accepting it until after her fourteenth birthday.

She accepted the dirt, she accepted the listless attitude of her mother, she accepted the other children and didn't think much about it. When there was a collection of dirty crockery filling the sink and she was told to wash it, she did. Not with any eagerness to make order out of chaos but because she was told to and if she didn't she was inviting a clip. She had no evangelical urge to lift her family out of their eternal state of squalor, at the time she knew little else, for most of the families she knew lived in much the same conditions. Dirty crockery remained on the table until it had to be washed, beds were

14

made when they were too muddled to get into and floors were only cleaned on rare occasions. Slum conditions seldom breed good housekeepers and if there were any around Gloria didn't know them.

It was about six months after her fourteenth birthday that Gloria stopped accepting. She came home from school one day and there was no sign of her mother or little Gary. The other children were not yet home, no doubt playing somewhere. Tom Craddock was sitting at the kitchen table, his shirt open, showing his big, hairy chest. There was a litter of dirty crockery on the table and a couple of empty bottles. A full glass of beer foamed in front of him.

'You've come 'ome early f'once.' He grinned, showing yellow but strong teeth.

'So 'ave you,' she answered, indifferent.

'Felt ill and come back. You'd better get them things washed up.'

'Wash 'em yerself. I'm going to find Ma.' Gloria had no particular yearning for her mother's company but it was better than her stepfather's. She wanted to get away from him but she wasn't sure why.

'You do as you're told, you young bitch, and it isn't any good looking for yer ma. She's gorn to the pictures and taken Gary.'

'Well, I'm going out, too.' She went

towards the door but Tom Craddock was quicker. He caught her by the arm and kicked the door shut.

'Oo the 'ell do you think you are, going out w'en it suits you, comin' 'ome w'en it suits you. Cheeky little bastard after I kep' you all these years.'

Gloria was skinny but tall for her age and her face was almost on a level with his. She glared at him.

'Let me go, you silly old bugger. I'm not a kid anymore and if I don't want to do nothing I ain't goin' to.' It was the first time she had dared to cheek him and she didn't know why she was doing it now unless she instinctively knew there was something different about him.

'So you're not a kid any more, well, we'll soon prove that.' He let go of her arm and caught her round the shoulders, one clumsy, hairy hand began to feel her small, firm breast. 'Getting quite a tasty bit, just right for a bit o' fun.'

She didn't scream, she was caught by a mixture of anger, fear and surprise. She stared at him with wide eyes while his hand continued to fumble with her breasts then, suddenly, his hand went down and pulled up her frock, his face came down on hers and her glasses were knocked off. It was then that she

16

bit him and as she tasted the blood from his full lip she let go and spat at him. He let go of her, put his hand to his mouth and a torrent of oaths poured out. She stood for a moment, staring at him and when she spoke her voice was so quiet she hardly recognised it.

'You dirty, filthy, old bastard. You won't never get the chance to touch me like that again and you'd better tell Ma 'ow you got that bite w'en she comes in.'

She stooped to pick up her glasses, saw they were broken and left them on the floor. As she went out of the room and closed the door he panicked.

'Come back, you little fool,' he shouted, 'come back, I didn't mean nothing.'

She was halfway down the stairs. She turned and gave him a look which was full of childish outrage and contempt. Once in the street she didn't know where to go but she would not go back there, ever. She walked for hours and somewhere around midnight she turned a corner and walked smack into someone she would have avoided if she could. A large copper. He caught her by the arm and asked her where she was off to. Lilac Grove and district considered coppers their natural enemies. She told him to mind his own business but it didn't work. Neither would she tell him where she lived.

'Then you'd better come along to the station.'

She tried to pull away but the grip on her arm was too strong. She went with him, her face sullen. In the station he handed her over to a policewoman. She drank the tea and ate the cheese sandwich a burly policeman brought but refused to say where she lived or give her name. The policewoman sighed. These kids, what could you do with them. They gave her a bed in a cell and locked her in. Whoever she was she was in need of care and protection.

In the morning she was told that if she didn't tell them who she was she would have to go before the juvenile court. Her eyes looked strangely defenceless without her glasses.

'But I ain't done nothing.'

'You're too young to be wandering the streets at midnight. We want to know who your parents are and why they weren't taking more care of you.'

The look Gloria gave the policewoman was near despair but at last the story came out and after all the preliminaries she was taken into care.

The next two years in the home were not perfection but they were better than Lilac Grove although Gloria missed Celia and

Gary. She sang in the choir, worked well at school, wasn't the slightest good at games but was amazingly capable at housework in spite of her beginnings and she was no trouble to anyone. Perhaps it was because of her musical ear that her spoken English improved by leaps and bounds. They kept her at the school until she was seventeen and during all that time her mother never came to see her. If she cared about this she never showed it. She showed no particular bent except for housework and cooking so the inevitable happened. She became mother's help to a vicar and his wife who had two small children. They knew she was a treasure and told her so. She warmed towards them and worked twice as hard. Those early years in Lilac Grove seemed to have had no effect apart from the fact that she renounced the name of Gloria and asked to be called Janie. A point for which the vicar's wife was grateful.

It was the vicar who persuaded her to go to the youth club. After the first night there he wondered if she was going to exchange working in the vicarage for working in the youth club for she was happier helping with the refreshments rather than mixing with the other youngsters. She was far too quiet. The Johnsons didn't know if she was self-

19

conscious over her background or just shy. With the children she was different, gay and playful and they adored her. In the playroom there was an old record player and a pile of old records.

'See if you can get her to sing with the group,' Charlotte Johnson said to her husband. 'She's got a charming voice.'

If it hadn't been for Kathy, who played the drums, Janie might not have given in but Kathy had a persuasive way. There were five of them and they all knew music and Janie learnt as she went along. She was eighteen when Roger Phillips came to stay at Hillingford Heath for a few days. He was in his early twenties, a professional pianist and when he heard Janie sing he was impressed. He had the good sense to talk to the Johnsons first and tell them she should have a chance to use her voice. The Johnsons were not fools and it said a lot for Roger that they were sure of his integrity. He took Janie to Arnold Banstead and that was how Janie Smith was born.

The Johnsons hated to part with her but they gave her the push she needed and told her it didn't mean the vicarage was not still her home.

She didn't sail immediately to the top. There was a year of uncertainty in which she worked in a shop and sang with a dance band when they wanted her while Roger coached her and Banstead got her occasional work. Then she cut her first disc. That was when Roger knew she was different. The disc was good and Roger was excited. He took her in his arms, hugged her and kissed her soundly. She pulled away from him, her eyes blazing, then she smacked his face.

'Don't you ever do that again. I won't be touched by anyone, ever!'

Her fury was out of all proportion to the offence. He stared at her in astonishment, shrugged his shoulders and said he was sorry. At that time he knew nothing of her background apart from the fact that she was an orphan.

Now she lay in the hot bath and wondered if Roger was right and having Celia with her was a very big mistake. Would she ever be more than a little slut? Had it been stupid ever to go back to Lilac Grove? Roger had said at the time that she was out of her mind but she couldn't explain that the period she had been with the Johnsons and the close association with them since, had given her a sense of duty she didn't think she could have learnt from anyone else. The time in the home hadn't done it. There she had just been glad she was away from Tom Craddock and the filth. The Johnsons were different. They had a spirit of loving kindness to everyone. They were tolerant and understanding. The sympathy and gentleness they had shown to the bad-tempered old aunt who had come to live with them impressed her deeply. It was much more than duty. They were marvellous in her eyes. She had talked to them about doing something for her own family and they had agreed. Roger had been dead against it. She didn't know that when she had smacked his face he had gone to the Johnsons and told them. Frank Johnson had explained why she had been taken into care. It was that knowledge which made him even more argumentative about helping her family.

'You are a fool to think of doing anything for them,' he said. 'They'll batten on to you like leeches once they know how well you are doing.'

'Don't be an idiot, Roger. I'm no fool. I'll do what I can but only if they stay away from me. Frank and Charlotte agree I may be able to do something for the younger ones.'

'Frank and Charlotte see the world through rose-coloured spectacles.'

He went and saw them but Frank smiled.

'You've known Janie three years now, Roger, and you should realise her strength of character. Are you in love with her by any chance?'

22

Roger gave a sudden grin. 'I'm fond of her but she keeps me at a distance. She keeps all men at a distance. There's an icy core in our Janie which I defy anyone to thaw. The maddening thing is that I've been in love with other girls, warm, ordinary girls. I nearly asked one to marry me but, damn the monkey-faced brat, her face came between us. Silly, isn't it?'

'Why on earth do you always call her monkey face? She's a good looking young woman.'

'She reminds me of the three monkeys. "Hear no evil, see no evil, speak no evil." She is indifferent to what people might think or say. She'll ask me in in the small hours for a cup of tea regardless of whether it might give her a reputation, but I can't see any man taking liberties with her.'

'And therein lies her strength. Janie is good.'

'Or hasn't any feelings.'

'That's not true and you know it. Let her do what she thinks is right. She won't be happy if she doesn't but I must admit I'd rather she didn't see much of them.'

So Janie went to Lilac Grove and told her mother she would do what she could. She was twenty-one then, very quiet and dignified. Craddock was out and she was thankful. The memory of him always made her feel sick. But Celia was there, a gawky thirteen but showing promise of great beauty.

'If you come near me I won't give you a penny.' She looked at her mother, now more sluttish than ever.

Going there had been a mistake and she didn't repeat it but she sent money regularly. It was Celia who stayed in her mind. Not the Celia she knew now but the child she had been. Then three months ago she had arrived on the doorstep. Flashily dressed and over-made-up. She said she had been working in a factory, her father had taken all her money and she couldn't stay at home any more. Janie took her inside and told her to sit down and tell the truth. Celia looked at her with big blue eyes that suddenly filled with tears.

'Well, they didn't get all the bloody money out of me. They didn't know how much I got but it isn't that. The old man can't keep his hands to himself, you know that, and I'm not standing for it. I hadn't anywhere to go except here.'

Janie felt sick although even then she didn't know how much was truth and how much lies. He was a filthy old devil but would he try the same thing with his own child as he did with her? She didn't know and she couldn't let the girl go back. It might be true.

24

'I only want to stay long enough to get another job and a room.'

Janie saw the quick, avid glance of those blue eyes round the room. She was envious but wasn't that natural? She was a young girl and naturally she wanted pretty things.

'You can stay and later we'll decide what to do but first you need some clothes.' She looked at the small case by Celia's side. The sooner she had her settled in the better.

She spoke far better than Janie had done when she left home and she was quick, with a shrewd, cockney quickness. She accepted the simple clothes Janie bought for her and allowed her hair to be cut in a swinging bob and obediently let herself be enrolled in a secretarial college. For two or three weeks all was well. Celia looked like being a nice little sister. Then one night Janie came home to find the kitchen a shambles. Celia must have been entertaining.

'Only some of the girls from the school. You don't mind, do you! I'm afraid they didn't go until after Fanny was in bed.' They hadn't even been there when Fanny went to bed.

A few nights later Janie spilt coffee on her dress. As a rule she had three changes with her but on this occasion only two. There was plenty of time to get home and back and she loved driving. The lights were on in the studio and when she went in a boy was sprawled on the settee, Celia was standing, cool and self-possessed, by the record player. Janie had a nasty feeling she hadn't been standing there long and Fanny was out. The boy stared at her insolently and made no attempt to get up. Janie felt her temper rising. This was something she would not have.

'Get out, now!' He went but the look he gave her was telling. Celia was no innocent.

'Don't you dare bring a man in this house again.'

'I suppose it's different when it's your precious Roger.' Celia was showing her true colours. Janie lost all self-control and smacked the girl's face.

'Roger and I work together and that is all.'

'Nice work!' Celia held her hand to her reddened cheek. 'Don't you touch me again or I'll make you pay.' Suddenly she seemed to come to her senses. 'I'm sorry, Janie, I didn't mean it and there wasn't any harm in him coming here, really. I was just fed up. I'll never make a secretary. What I want is to be a singer and I can sing. If only you'd let me have the chance.'

'I've no time to talk about it now. I only came back to get another dress. I'll see you in

26

the morning.'

She certainly had looks. Did she have a voice? Get Roger to hear her. He was a wonderful judge.

In the morning he played for her and Janie listened with something close to disgust. In that song all her cheapness came over. She looked what she could so easily be. A little tart.

'Sorry, kid, your voice is not good enough, even with training.' Roger spoke with self-restraint. 'You'd never make another Janie.'

'Who said I wanted to? Do you think I'd be content to be what she is. I'd make the top!' She spoke with complete self-confidence and, now she was sure Roger had no intention of helping her, dropped all pretensions. Her eyes turned to Janie. 'Oh, I know what's wrong with you! You're just—' the word she used was far from pretty, 'jealous. Scared little sister is a bloody sight better than you are.'

'Don't talk rubbish, Celia. Janie has no need to be jealous. She's in a class of her own. You'd never make it if you tried till doomsday. Get on with your secretarial course and make a go of it.'

Janie didn't speak, she was beginning to wonder if Celia went near the school and she had no idea what she did all day. Celia's eyes were bright with anger.

'Crap! You don't want me to get into the business. Don't worry, I'll make the headlines just the same.' She went out of the studio with her head in the air.

'You've got a tiger there. What about letting Banstead hear her? His opinion might cure some of her cockiness.'

'No!' The word came out sharply. 'I couldn't bear it. There's something nasty about her singing.'

Since then things had gone from bad to worse and it seemed that Celia won every battle. At least she brought no one else home which was something to be thankful for.

Sleep refused to come and in the morning Janie felt more tired than when she went to bed. It seemed that she had lived all her life over again in the last hours. Fanny brought up her tea and drew back the curtains.

'It's a miserable morning and you look as if you haven't slept.' Fanny was fat and forty and adored Janie. 'Been worrying about that little minx again, I suppose. She may be your sister but you'll never do anything with her and the best thing you can do is to send her about her business.'

'How can I, Fanny? She's only a kid.'

'Kid indeed. She's a whole lot older than you. One of these days I'll tan her backside

28

for her.'

'What has she been up to now?'

'Nothing in particular.' Fanny suddenly grinned. 'It's just her, her manner, her cheek and the way when she is in she is always on the phone. And you can bet your life it's always a man. Oh, perhaps I'm just narked. She's making things difficult for you.'

What took Janie's breath away was her ability to pull the wool over other people's eyes when it suited her. With her and Roger and Fanny she no longer bothered but when Arnold Banstead came she was another girl. Celia had been unassuming, sweet and listening. Banstead saw her outstanding beauty which was brought out by the simple clothes Janie had bought her.

'It's nice to meet Janie's little sister. Are you going to be a singer, too?'

'No, Janie thinks it would be better if I become a secretary.'

'She's probably right, my dear. Janie is wise.'

'Yes, I know.' It was said with what could have been admiration but Janie saw the malice in the blue eyes. 'It would be different if I had as much talent as Janie.' The voice that could be shrill and penetrating was wistful.

'Can you sing?'

'A little, but Janie doesn't think it is good enough to get me anywhere.'

'I must hear you some time.'

'That's kind of you but I don't want to do anything Janie doesn't want me to do.'

'Well, that's a change!' Janie was boiling.

Arnold Banstead looked at her in surprise. Was she afraid this lovely young sister would outdistance her?

There were other people to whom Celia had given the same treatment. Always influential ones. She was two people, showing whichever character she wished. She had Janie in a cleft stick and was laughing in triumph. Janie knew that she had come to her in order to get all she could out of her and to get into show business. To send her packing now would make it worse. Celia would make sure of that. If only she had had the sense to help her family through someone else.

On Monday morning there was a recording session. Arnold's greeting was not so warm as usual and Janie felt it. Damn Celia! There was nothing she was not spoiling.

'How's that lovely young sister of yours, Janie?'

'Quite well.' Her voice was cold.

'Can she sing?'

'You'd better ask Roger. He's heard her.'

'Her voice has the quality of a cat.' Roger

laughed. He had nearly added, 'An alley cat!' but couldn't for Janie's sake. Dear Janie with that warm, vibrant voice but that cool, withdrawn air that said, 'Don't touch me!' He had an odd feeling that she was willing to give her voice, which was almost her whole self, her soul, but her body must remain inviolate. It was almost sacrilege to think of her as Celia's sister. There had been one occasion when he had arrived at Janie's before she was ready to rehearse. Celia was in the studio and while he sorted music she had stood close, making sure he could feel the pressure of her firm, full breast against his arm. He was no prude but the brazen invitation made him furious. Celia was a nasty piece of work and he wished he knew how Janie could get rid of her without any trouble but he began to doubt it. Celia was becoming more of a menace every day. Somebody ought to strangle her!

Arnold looked from one to the other. 'Are you sure you haven't made a mistake?'

'No, why?' Roger was puzzled. Arnold usually accepted his judgment.

'Because Neville Neilson has her in tow. She told him she is your sister, Janie.'

Janie stared at him and her eyes glittered with anger. Arnold's grew wide with astonishment. Cool, quiet Janie who seldom showed any feeling except for her singing was

31

in such a cold fury she looked almost dangerous. Was it because the girl had used her name or just jealousy? Or was it because the girl had said she didn't want to do anything Janie didn't want her to do and then gone to Neilson behind her back? Why had Celia lied? Was she afraid of Janie? The thoughts chased themselves round while Janie stood quite still, her eyes emerald green in her thin, white face. She was too thin, as if her body didn't know how to love. God damn it, why was he thinking like this? He had always had a warm feeling for Janie. It was as if that lovely little creature was there, putting the thoughts into his head.

When Janie spoke her voice was the tinkle of breaking glass.

'I can't record today. I'm going home to see that little bitch.'

It was the first time Arnold had ever heard Janie say anything not absolutely correct. Her perfect manners often tickled his sense of humour, she was like a girl from a good and old-fashioned finishing school. Roger was quietly lighting a cigarette.

'Come along, Janie, forget it and get on with the job. Celia's not you and whatever she does it can't make any difference to you unless you let it.'

Janie drew on her gloves. 'I'm going home.

I'll be at the Pelican on time.'

'Now why,' said Arnold as the door closed behind her, 'did she go off like that? It would have been so much more sensible to let me hear her in the first place. Why have her to live with her at all if she feels like that?'

'That's Janie's business. Well, no recording. You can tell the boys it's off. I might as well go home myself.'

Arnold wished he hadn't seen Janie in such a rage and later he wished it even more.

CHAPTER TWO

Janie drove home in a white fury. She cut in on traffic and ignored indignant horns. Her one ambition was to get home and give Celia the length of her tongue. Neville Neilson of all people. The man who had done his damndest to get her away from Arnold Banstead. Arnold didn't know about it but she was certain that Celia did. Neilson wanted to get even with her. He had come to see her with an offer and it was a very good one. Tall, elegant, the perfect gentleman. She told him Banstead was her agent and he said it could be done through him if she wished.

I must have been green, she thought, as she just scraped past the traffic lights. As if he had any intention of letting Arnold in on it. Within a few minutes she was sure of that.

She had been standing by the piano. He came over and stood near her and she didn't move away. That would have looked as if she was scared and never in her life would she show that.

'I'll give you a far better deal than Banstead and I know your contract isn't binding.'

'So you don't believe in a gentleman's agreement?'

'Not in business and I can give you far more.'

The look in his eyes put her on her guard.

'You've nothing I want, Mr Neilson.'

'Don't be so sure. I can put you right on top.'

He meant it. Thought she was wasting herself. It was a long time since he had seen anyone with such promise. She should be learning languages. Paris would go crazy about her. She was different. Cool and withdrawn but a hint of fire underneath. Perhaps it was the coolness of her smile that made him lose his common sense. Normally he liked to be sure a woman was willing before he made overtures. This time he didn't wait. He caught her in his arms partly in fun but she didn't know that.

'You've got everything it takes, Janie Smith, and I like to see talent made the most of.'

He half expected her to pull away but she stood quite still until he put his face down to hers and then all hell was let loose.

'You filthy scum!' Her long nails scratched his face deeply. 'Go home and tell your wife how you got that! I shall tell Arnold how you tried to doublecross him and if I have one more suggestion from you I'll make your name stink.'

He put his handkerchief to his face and grinned. Neville Neilson had the morals of a tomcat but he could laugh at himself as well as at other people.

'I don't happen to have a wife so there will be no need for a confession, and as for Banstead, you can tell him what you like. If he has any sense he'll do more for you than he's doing. I'd still put you right on top if you'd let me but don't think it would be for favours. I like my women willing.'

Janie didn't believe him and she was sure that if ever he could do her a dirty turn he would. Now Celia had given him that chance. He'd coach her and make her headline news all right. She could see the results. Put her in one of the dirtiest nightclubs in town and bill her as Janie Smith's little sister. With fury unabated she drove up to the house. Celia was sitting in the studio smoking. She looked up as Janie came into the room and her smile was venomous.

'It didn't take long for the news to reach you and you don't like it much, do you? Well, let me tell you this, Neville Neilson is going to put me right at the top of the tree, higher than you'll ever get for all your airs and graces.'

'He'll get you to the top all right, you little fool.' Janie's voice was clear as crystal with a quality that carried and it was full of biting anger. 'Haven't you enough sense to know that all he wants is to hurt me. And the top rung he'll put you on won't be where I am. The top of some filthy club where men go for kicks. You've no talent for anything else.'

'What you mean is you don't want me to think I have any talent, don't want me to get anywhere.' There was a sudden change in Celia's voice. It rang out passionately and yet it sounded hurt and unhappy. Why, Janie asked herself, why?

'You've been jealous of me ever since I put a foot in the door. You've never wanted to help me but I think you're afraid I may tell about the time that Roger leaves in the morning. Well, I wouldn't do that, I wouldn't spoil your reputation although you've tried to spoil my chances. You don't want me to sing because you know I could be a lot better than you. All you have wanted is to convince me I'm no good and make a secretary of me.'

It was then that the floodgates were opened and Janie called her little sister all the things she learnt when she lived in Lilac Grove. But even while she was giving vent to an almost ungovernable rage she knew there was something wrong. Celia had been using the wrong words, words that didn't ring true, she was acting a part, her voice sounded tearful but it didn't stop the spiteful curl of her lips. Janie knew that in some way Celia was making a fool out of her and it increased her anger.

'Get out of here, you filthy little bitch, before I wring your neck. All you're fit for is bed and I wouldn't mind betting you've had your share of that.'

She didn't touch the girl but she longed to. Longed to slap the malicious mouth, to take her by the shoulders and shake her, wanted to hurt her as much as she had been hurt on that horrible day that Celia's father had touched her own childish body. In Celia she could see Tom Craddock with all his nastiness.

Celia went, hips swinging, high, firm breasts thrust forward. Janie went limp and slumped in a chair, rage subsiding and sick memory taking its place. It was if she could again feel Tom Craddock's hands on her budding breasts. She knew now what made her different. It wasn't Lilac Grove or the knowledge she was a bastard. It was the sick feeling of disgust that her young, childish body had been touched by the obscenity of those clawing hands. Something had been wrenched from her in those moments that she would never get back. It had taken Celia's nastiness to give her the truth. She had pushed it out of her mind for so long but now she deliberately thought about it, like feeling a sore place to see if it still hurt. The time with the Johnsons had been a healing period but the wound had only healed on the surface, underneath it was still raw. Not for her the happiness of being in love because if ever she found herself in a man's arms it would be Tom Craddock leering down at her. She would never be free of the sickness, never. Tears poured down her cheeks.

The door opened and Fanny came in with a tray.

'What you need is a good strong cup of coffee. Where is that limb of Satan? Gone to her room now she's done as much damage as she can?'

'It's all right, Fanny. I'll get over it but I could have cheerfully wrung her neck.'

'It's not just what she said to you!'

'What else?' The tears were still falling down Janie's thin cheeks and Fanny thought she had lost a lot of weight since her sister had been with them. Not that Fanny thought of Celia as Janie's sister. More often than not it was 'that young hell-cat!'

'That dratted Mrs. Simmons came over. Wanted to borrow some sugar. She's always borrowing something although I will say she always returns it.' Mrs. Simmons was housekeeper to the business couple next door.

'Candidly I don't think she really wants to borrow anything. Just wants to find out the latest. She came round the back way and that young devil was in the garden. Of course she had to ask her why she wasn't at college. Never says school, that one.'

'What did Celia say?'

'Told her she had left because she was going into show business. All sweetness and light, she was, but as if that wasn't enough she went on to tell her that she didn't want to upset you because you wanted her to be a secretary so that she could work for you but, after all, it was her future. She even shed a few tears.'

'Dear God, how could she?'

'Then you have to lose your temper! I thought that woman had gone but when I looked out of the window she was standing outside listening. I was so mad I asked her if she had nothing better to do than to listen to a private conversation. Conversation!' Fanny's broad face broke into a grin. 'I've never heard you use language like that before. You must have given her a few new words but I wish she hadn't heard. She's a nasty gossip.'

'And I bet Celia knew she was there but it's done now and the best thing we can do is forget it.'

'And send that little devil packing.'

'I can't do that but I should never have let her stay in the first place. I might have known it would cause trouble. Roger said it would.'

'And he's got his head well screwed on.' She poured the coffee and gave Janie a cup. 'I thought you were supposed to be recording.'

'I should be but Arnold told me that Celia was being taken under Neville Neilson's wing and I was so mad I came back to have it out with her. I should have got on with my job and put her out of my mind.'

'Mr. Banstead will get over it. It's the first time you've let anyone down since I've been with you and that is more than four years.'

'And I don't know what I would do without you.'

'The doing isn't all on one side. The best thing you can do is to go and lie down.'

Janie didn't see Celia before she went to The Purple Pelican. Roger was waiting in her dressing room.

'Feeling better?'

She screwed up her short, too broad nose and gave him the grin she reserved for her friends.

'Much! God, how I blew my top. I could have brained the little beast. I wonder if she found out about Neville Neilson.'

'What do you mean, found out about him?'

41

She told Roger the story but now it sounded rather silly. Roger gave her an amused smile.

'So that's why you are always so frigidly polite to him! He's shrewd but I don't think he is quite as bad as you think. Just trying it on, hopefully. Did you ever tell Arnold?'

'Good lord, no! What would have been the point?'

'None I suppose.'

Janie was feeling much better. Somehow she would have to sort things out tomorrow but tonight she would put it right out of her head. At eleven she was off until half past twelve. She went to her dressing room and locked the door. Once someone tapped but she didn't answer. She needed to rest. She wasn't going to let Celia mess up her career and tonight there was no sign of that happening. She was at her best and she could feel it. Her voice warm and sweet with the faint trace of huskiness which was so appealing. Roger had never heard her so good. The audience adored her and after her last number, Ted Baynes, the proprietor, begged her to go back.

'Give them anything, some of the old ones. I must see Arnold before you go to America. It's your first time overseas, isn't it. They'll eat you.'

When at last they let her go she went back to her dressing room. Ted was waiting for her.

'Have you fallen in love or something? I've never heard you put it across so well.'

Unexpected tears trickled down her cheeks. 'No, nothing like that.' Then she giggled. 'I've been through an emotional upheaval and I thought I shouldn't get through the evening. Now I begin to wonder if losing my temper is good for my performance.'

'Be an angel and have supper on the floor with Roger. They'll love to see you.'

Usually she went home as soon as she was free but tonight she didn't want to. This was more like home at the moment than the house at Hampstead and yet she loved it dearly. It was her first real home and she had furnished it with loving care. Until two years ago she had lived in a flat and the house was something special. Celia had taken away the joy. When Roger and she went to their table there was a round of applause. She raised her hand and smiled, wanting to take them all to her heart. Celia didn't matter. She had made her own niche and if her sister made one for herself, even in the sleaziest nightclub, she didn't care a damn. Nothing could touch her if she could move people like this.

She ate the minutest amount of food and

Roger watched her anxiously.

'You don't eat enough to keep a fly alive.'

'Rubbish. I like Fanny's cooking better than this.'

'Then I hope you do it justice. You were great tonight. I've lost my fears that that little devil would mess up your career. You were wonderful.'

'Thank you, Roger. If it wasn't for you I wouldn't be here at all. I won't let you down.'

The smile she gave him was warm and gentle. She wasn't the snow maiden, after all. There was strength and depth to her character. Frank Johnson was right. That brute of a stepfather had chilled her so that it would take continual tenderness to overcome her fears. It wasn't coldness, just fear of physical contact. He realised now that he loved her with a deep enduring love in spite of flirtations with other women, in spite of once being on the verge of proposing to one. He wanted to lean across the table and say, 'Hi, monkey face, I've made a great discovery. I love you and want to marry you.' Instead he said, 'Come along, for goodness' sake eat a little more or the patrons will think there is something wrong with the food.'

'I'm not hungry. The applause filled me right up, to here.' She put her hand to her thin neck.

An elderly man stopped by the table to thank her for her performance. She looked up at him and her smile was full of gratitude. He was a short, thick-set northerner with a balding, bullet head and kind eyes. He walked on and Janie looked at Roger.

'I'd like to have had a father like that. Warm and kind and very gentle.'

'I wish you had known mine. He was like that. My parents weren't clever but they were the best parents in the world.'

'They're both dead?'

'Yes, before I met you.' All these years and she had never shown any interest before. It gave him a warm glow. She was beginning to see him as something more than a figure at the piano. Then she shattered the glow.

'You should get married, Roger. You'd make a wonderful father and that's what kids need. It doesn't matter if there isn't much money as long as they are loved and wanted.'

'And what about you? Isn't it time you thought of getting married?'

She giggled. '"Nobody asked me, sir, she said." No, I'm not the marrying kind. I'm better on my own. You know what they say. "He travels fastest who travels alone." It's the only way if you want to get to the top.'

'And that's what you want to do?'

'Yes. I do now. The strange thing is that

until today I was afraid. The higher you climb the farther you fall but I won't fall.'

'But those Olympian heights may be cold and lonely.'

'I shan't let that worry me.'

She was warmer, different, but she was also stronger, as if she suddenly knew where she was going. He wished the warmth were for him but he could wait.

'Want me to drive you home? I can collect my car tomorrow.'

'No, that's all right. Besides, I don't want a cuppa tonight.' She smiled. 'I shall go straight to bed and dream of what a lovely evening it has been.'

He saw her to her car. 'Good night, monkey face. Here's to those sweet dreams. He longed to bend down and kiss her cheek but no, give her time, lots of time. The thaw had begun but better not show how he was feeling, not yet.

Janie drove home slowly. Once away from the Pelican she was a coward again. Afraid that when she went upstairs she would hear the click of Celia's latch. The unquiet presence that took the peace from the house. Perhaps she would make a cup of tea, after all. She went straight through to the kitchen. Everything was in perfect order. How was it that so often when she came home Celia was

46

awake? Was she just a light sleeper and always heard the car?

She made herself a cup of tea and sat drinking it, trying to make some sort of plans for the future, remembering Celia as a four-year-old with china-blue eyes and pale, honey-gold hair. Rose-bud mouth, delicate nose with flaring nostrils, high cheek-bones, gently tinted. A child with the looks of a cherub. A doll to be pampered and petted and shielded from the others. She hadn't realised that even then Celia had always managed to get round her. Anything she ever had if Celia wanted it she got it. Why hadn't she remembered that? Celia was as brutal, cunning and lewd as her own father.

She couldn't keep her here but neither could she just turn her out. Oh, lord, the best thing to do was to sleep on it and perhaps tomorrow a solution would come. Tonight had been the best ever and she wasn't going to spoil it by worrying.

There was no sound from Celia's door. Had her display of temper made her sister wary? She had reached the top of the stairs and the sudden memory of Mrs Simmons listening to her colourful language struck her sense of humour. Tonight nothing was going to upset her. Her latest thriller! She left it in the studio and she always like to read for half an hour. She went down the stairs again, softly humming her latest number. Switching on the light she glanced round but the book was not on the table where she thought she had left it. Perhaps she had taken it upstairs after all. Or maybe Fanny had. Fanny had gone to her sister for the night and she always made sure everything was in order before she left. But there was something different. The settee, usually against the wall, had been pulled round to the fireplace and one bar of the fire was on. It wasn't till then that she noticed Celia's bright head resting on the arm. Damn the girl, she would have to wake her up and switch off the fire. For a moment she was tempted to leave her there. No, better wake her up.

She walked over to the settee and was just going to put her hand on her shoulder when she saw the protruding eyes and open mouth. She put her hand to her own mouth and stifled a scream. For several moments she stood in horrified silence. Then she stumbled to the telephone and dialled Roger's number.

CHAPTER THREE

Roger was tired but feeling far happier about Janie. He was sure something could be worked out over Celia. Janie had been an idiot to take the girl in but Janie was Janie and he didn't want her different. Underneath the cool façade he knew there was warmth and love even if it took a devil of a time to get down to it. There was no doubt in his mind that Frank Johnson was right and fear was the cause of that reserve. He got into bed thinking how lucky it was that her first job had been with the Johnsons. Perhaps orphanages were human!

He fell asleep immediately and was vastly indignant when a persistent 'Burr-burr' dragged him back to consciousness. He stretched out a hand and pulled the receiver from its cradle and wondered who the dickens would be calling at such an hour. Janie's voice startled him. For a moment he had failed to recognise it for it was little more than a whisper.

'Please, Roger, can you come round?'

'What's wrong, monkey face, you sound upset?' That, he thought, was the understatement of the year. She sounded terrified.

'Don't tell me that little sister of yours is on the warpath again. I'll come round and tell her to go to hell.'

'I can't tell you anything on the phone, Roger, but please come quickly.'

He got into his clothes and wondered what on earth the little devil had done now. He hadn't any doubt it was Celia. If he had anything to do with it he would turn her out now, bag and baggage. It was four-thirty when he reached the house and as he stopped the car Janie opened the door and he saw she was still dressed and her make-up not yet washed off. There was no sign of tears but her eyes were wide and her face white as a ghost. He ran up the steps and put a light arm round her shoulders and she made no resistance.

'What is it, monkey face? You look all in. Come and sit down and I'll make you a cuppa.'

She shook her head. 'No, come into the studio.' Her voice no longer shook but she sounded even more frightened than she had on the phone. She led him straight to the settee and he stared in horror at Celia's distorted face. There was no trace of the beauty that had been. The limp hand hanging loosely to the floor looking infinitely pathetic, which was more than he had ever thought when she was alive.

'Dear God, when did you find her?'

'I was going up to bed but remembered I had left my book down here and came to fetch it. Then I saw her.'

'You've phoned the police?'

She looked at him with bewildered eyes and shook her head.

'I just rang you.'

'All right, dear, don't worry, I'll call them.' It wasn't any use telling her she should have called them first, clearly she hadn't even thought about it. He asked them to come at once and said there had been a murder.

'What makes you say it is a murder, sir.'

'You'd hardly strangle yourself with a scarf, would you?'

'Hardly, sir. The address?'

He took Janie into the kitchen and put on the kettle. Apart from the deathly white of her face she was quite calm.

'I don't want any tea. I made myself one when I came in and had a cigarette.'

He switched off the kettle and fetched her a stiff whisky. A few minutes later the police arrived. He took them into the studio and showed them Celia's body.

'You know who she is, sir?' The sergeant looked at him with a basilisk stare.

'Of course I do. It's Celia, Janie Smith's young sister.'

'And did you find her?'

'Of course not. Janie found her.'

'Then why was it you rang?'

'Janie rang me and asked me to come round. She should have rung you but she was too shocked to think straight.'

'Of course, sir, I understand. I take it you are a friend of the family.'

'I'm Janie's accompanist. She's a singer.'

'That Janie Smith! I've heard some of her records. Now may I see her?'

'You'd better come into the kitchen. I've given her a drink.' There was a ring at the door.

'That'll be the doctor. My man will let him in.'

Janie told them briefly what had happened. When she said she had made herself a cup of tea the sergeant looked round expectantly. Almost as if he had asked her she said, 'I washed up and put everything away. I always do. Fanny, that's my housekeeper, always keeps everything so tidy.'

'And where is she, miss, or doesn't she sleep in?'

'Yes but tonight she's gone to see her married sister and won't be back until the morning.'

52

'You must have been in half an hour or so before you knew your sister was dead.'

'I suppose so. I didn't look at the time.'

'And there was no sign of anyone having broken in?'

'I didn't look, I didn't think about it.'

One of the constables had already taken a quick look round and said there was no sign of breaking and entering. The sergeant looked at Janie. It was then that she made her first silly statement.

'Celia said she was going to make the headlines.'

'What do you mean by that, miss?'

'She wanted to be a singer and I said she was no good but she said she would be and she'd make the headlines. It seems a long time ago but only this morning she said she'd get to the top of the tree.'

'Do you mean you quarrelled?'

Roger laid a hand on her arm, suddenly alarmed by the expression on the sergeant's face, but it was too late. Janie was unconscious of saying the wrong thing.

'I'm afraid we did. I was pretty angry.'

'I'll go in and see what the doctor says.'

'Janie, you shouldn't have told him you quarrelled.'

'Why not? It's true.' Then she looked at Roger's face. 'You don't think he thinks I did

53

it?' There was no fear in her eyes, just astonishment. 'But he couldn't. She was dead when I came in.'

'Of course she was but there was no need to say anything.'

When the sergeant came back there was a silk scarf in his hands.

'Have you seen this before, miss?'

'Of course, it's mine. Celia had a habit of borrowing my things. Anything that happened to be handy.'

'Do you mind telling me where you were between eleven p.m. and midnight last night?'

Janie looked bewildered and then seemed to understand. 'Oh, you mean tonight, but of course, it's morning now. Is that when Celia was killed?'

'I just want to know where you were.'

'At The Purple Pelican.'

'And you didn't leave there until you came home after your act?'

'No, when I was not singing I rested in my dressing room.'

It was a very long time before the house was free of policemen and then Janie refused to go to bed. She sat in the small lounge and Roger made cups of tea and cups of coffee and refused to leave until Fanny came home and took charge.

54

There was nothing in the morning papers but the evening ones carried the headlines Celia had said she would get.

'Unknown Killer in Nightclub Singer's House.'

'Janie Smith's Lovely Young Sister Strangled.'

And the rumours started to buzz. Janie stayed close to the house and refused to see anyone.

It was early afternoon when Roger pushed his way through the crowds and prayed it would only be a short time before they found whoever had murdered Celia. By the time the American tour started it would all be forgotten. In the meantime Ted had found someone to take Janie's place. Until after the funeral at least. That was the disadvantage of show business. There was always someone to take your place. Sometimes they weren't much good but sometimes they were and then it could be difficult to get back again. Who on earth had killed Celia and why? Someone she had met recently or someone from Lilac Grove? Roger wished Janie hadn't been so damn quick to tell that sergeant that she had quarrelled with Celia only that morning. In spite of the fact that she had been at the club when it happened it was easy to see how that man's mind worked and it wasn't pleasant.

Fanny opened the door and her face was grim.

'You'd better come into the kitchen. There's a damned plain-clothes inspector with her now. Questions and questions. You'd think it wasn't bad enough for her without all that nonsense.'

★   ★   ★

On Tuesday morning Inspector Henry Mason drove towards The Yard with his mind miles away. Had all gone as it should he and Beth would now be happily married and reclining on a sunny beach in the Canaries. Beth's brother Peter was her only close relative and naturally she wanted to postpone the wedding until he could be there but why, pondered Henry as he halted at the traffic lights, did he have to break his leg the day before he was due to board a plane for England? To Henry every day until he was married to Beth was a waste of time for they were not in the first flush of youth.

The car in front moved forward and Henry gave a sudden grin. Talk about love being for youth. The older you were the harder it hit you. He began to sing softly, 'It is when he thinks he's past love, it is then he meets his last love and he loves her as he's never loved

56

before!' Not that there had been much love before he met Beth. One or two abortive love affairs that had not touched him deeply. On a whole women did not take too kindly to a man who was liable to break a date at the last moment because his job had to be given priority. Henry had been very busy working his way up from a copper. There had been a time when he was in love with his cousin Sally but she had married Ian McCleod and later Henry realised his love had been a dream rather than love itself. Then, when he was certain he was a confirmed bachelor, he had met Beth while he was staying with Sally and Ian at Little Todsham. Beth, with rumpled, greying-fair curls and wide, friendly green eyes; Beth, with a smudge of paint on her cheek or clay on her fingers; Beth, with her quick laughter and warm, loving heart. Clever Beth, who could catch an unexpected expression on a face with a stroke of the brush or mould a lump of inanimate clay into a child's eager figure. What had he done to deserve her? Henry thought of himself as an ordinary copper doing what was often a dull and sometimes unpleasant job to the best of his ability. He never saw himself as The Wonder Boy, a title which was sometimes given him in derision and sometimes in admiration. It didn't impress Henry for he knew that there were many occasions in which he had been remarkably lucky.

There was nothing out of the ordinary in Henry's looks which was one thing that had helped to make him a good detective. He didn't stand out in a crowd. Only a little above average in height, with a good figure that pleased his tailor because it had no peculiarities. His jawline was strong and his teeth square and white. His brown hair showed no sign of thinning but it was greying at the temples. It was his eyes that Beth had noticed first. Large grey eyes with long, thick lashes. Eyes that were unexpectedly gentle in a man who was continually seeking out wrongdoers. On the other hand there were times when they could narrow and harden until those with a guilty conscience wished he would look in another direction.

Beth was now staying with a friend in north London and she and Henry were able to spend his off-duty time together and to both it was a revelation. Life was suddenly complete.

Henry was scarcely seated at his desk when Sergeant Price came in with the story of Celia Craddock's murder. It wasn't until he said that she was the sister of Janie Smith, the singer at The Purple Pelican, that Henry was jolted back to his job.

He had taken Beth to The Purple Pelican on Saturday. Normally it was far too expensive for Henry's pocket but it should have been their wedding day and therefore he was entitled to be extravagant. Mentally he digressed a moment to remember how gorgeous Beth had looked in green, her usually rumpled curls elegantly dressed and with glittery-green eye-shadow which made her green eyes sparkle. He also remembered how impressed they had both been by Janie Smith's performance and Beth saying, 'I'd like to do a portrait of her. Not because she is almost beautiful but because she has the look of a lost child. She hasn't yet found herself and I'd like to paint her before she does.' Stop thinking about Beth and concentrate on what Price is saying.

And Price, having said all he knew, ended with, 'Not much doubt about who did it. Her sister admits they quarrelled and she had plenty of opportunity.'

'How?' Henry's voice was non-committal. He thought of Janie Smith's eyes which were as green as Beth's but without the happy tranquillity. 'I thought she was at The Purple Pelican every evening. Half the night come to that.'

'I didn't see how she could at first but when I made inquiries it put a different complexion on it. The girl was probably killed between eleven and midnight. Time's a bit dicey at present. Waiting for a more detailed report. There was a bar of the electric fire on. Had the girl put it on because she was a bit chilly and the murderer forgot to switch it off or did the murderer put it on in the hope that it would confuse the time of death by delaying rigor mortis? Blasted criminals know too much these days. Hardly ever find a fingerprint that shouldn't be there and they know more about police methods than we do ourselves.' Price was the picture of gloom. 'But no one saw Janie Smith between eleven and half after midnight. The owner of the club admitted he'd knocked on her door at eleven-thirty and got no reply. He said he only knocked once and when she was resting she didn't always answer. He tried the door but it was locked. At that time the roads are pretty clear and I understand she is a good driver. She could have done the run easily in twenty minutes.'

'Could she have got out of the club and taken her car without being seen?'

'A bit tricky but it could have been done.'

'But even if they had had a quarrel why would she want to kill her sister and so stupidly? With her own scarf and all. It looks too simple to me.'

'Jealousy I should think. Her sister had been taken on by Neville Neilson. The chap who manages Esme. Show business people!' Price gave a sniff. 'Unbalanced lot, most of them.'

'That's a sweeping statement if ever I heard one!' Henry grinned. 'Doesn't seem enough motive for murder but you can never tell. What else have you found out?'

'You'd be surprised. The housekeeper next door heard the quarrel. Snooping type. Said she had just been to borrow some sugar and had spoken to the dead girl in the garden and she had told her that her sister didn't want her to be a singer. A few minutes later she heard the quarrel but, according to her, it was far more than that. She happened to be by the open window! She said Janie Smith's language was terrible and she threatened to strangle the girl. Her story is that she had spoken to the girl on several occasions and she was a sweet girl. She was about to tell me what she thought about Janie Smith but I cut her short.'

'What about parents?'

Price was suddenly disconcerted. He didn't know a thing about them.

'Didn't you ask her? Miss Smith, I mean.'

He was even more disconcerted. He hadn't.

61

'Well, we'd better find out, hadn't we? Of course there may be no parents. Has the girl always lived with her sister?'

'No, only the last three months.'

'We had better find out where she was before that.'

Henry was now sitting in the sunny studio in Janie's house. They had already been through Celia's belongings and could find no correspondence at all. There were a few snaps of her taken with other teenagers, with motor bikes and without. There was also well over a hundred pounds in one pound notes which Janie Smith said she had not given her and according to Celia she hadn't a penny when she came to her. Janie Smith sat on the arm of a chair and watched him with bright, unhappy eyes. They sparkled more brightly than most and he realised she was wearing contact lenses. When he asked if she had any parents she gave a brief nod.

'I take it you have already contacted them before they had chance to see it in the papers? The evening edition has it on the front page.'

'No.'

'But why? Surely it would be the natural thing to do?'

She gave him a faintly amused yet pathetic smile. 'If you knew my background you might have another opinion. I come from

Lilac Grove, down by the docks. At fourteen I was taken into care. I'm a bastard you see and my stepfather was not considered suitable. I haven't seen them for over three years.'

'Why has your sister been living with you these past three months? Apparently you didn't get on together.'

'She came to me with a story that could have been true and I didn't know what else to do. She was only a kid and I thought at first that I might be able to help. I was a fool. Celia was perfectly capable of standing on her own feet—and somebody else's—mostly mine since she has been here.'

'What about her friends?'

'I don't know anything about them. I don't believe she made any at the secretarial college I sent her to. I know that she only attended classes a few times and I haven't a clue what she did all day. At first I did think she was at classes. Once I came back between my turns and there was a boy of about twenty here, the street-corner type. I told him to get out and my sister that she was not to bring men in.'

'Did your housekeeper see him?'

'No, she was away for the night.'

'Did anyone else know you came home that night, Miss Smith?'

'I shouldn't think so. I'd spilt coffee down

one of my dresses and wanted another. If I had told Roger, he's my accompanist, he would have offered to come for me and he wouldn't know which dress to fetch and I didn't know for sure myself.'

So, she could slip out quite easily between her turns without being missed!

'Did you leave The Purple Pelican at all last night? Between when you arrived and when you left after your supper?' He was relaxed, easy, watching the smoke curl up from his cigarette as if he found that more important than his questions and her answers. 'Last night you went to your dressing room around eleven and Mr. Baynes says your door was locked when he went to speak to you. When he knocked you didn't answer.'

'Because I wanted to rest and didn't want to talk to anyone.'

'Were you tired or were you upset because of the quarrel with your sister?' He was still watching the smoke. 'It was a pretty bad quarrel, wasn't it? Do you mind telling me about it?'

'Oh, hell, do I have to go into details?' Briefly she told him. She also said she rested because she was determined not to spoil her singing. She had heard the knock and ignored it. Suddenly she smiled and Henry found himself warming to her but he wished she hadn't come home on that other evening between her numbers.

'Inspector, I wasn't only upset because I knew that Celia had made a fool of me but because I blew my top and completely reverted to the little kid from the slums. All my nice, ladylike façade slipped down the drain. I screamed like a fishwife and used language I thought I had forgotten. It was a shattering experience, believe me. I was not only furious with Celia but disgusted with myself.'

'Did you threaten to strangle her?'

'Quite possibly. I said the lot. I don't remember half of it now.'

'Did you know the housekeeper next door heard you?'

'Fanny told me. Poor pet, she was upset about that.'

'Weren't you?'

'Not particularly. I was too shocked at myself. It's over ten years since I left Lilac Grove. To find I was still the kid from the slums was not a nice experience.'

'I'm sure it wasn't but I shouldn't let it worry you.' He smiled and Jane was comforted, then suddenly, 'Miss Smith, did you kill your sister?' After that smile the words were cold and sharp and Janie looked at him in plain astonishment.

'Good heavens, no! In these last few weeks

I began to loathe her for what she was but I didn't have any reason to kill her even if I had wanted to and I can assure you I didn't.'

'In spite of the fact that she wanted to get ahead of you in show business?'

At this moment the door opened and Roger came in, his brown eyes almost red with anger. Henry looked at him with raised eyebrows. Janie introduced them and Roger glared.

'I should think Miss Smith has been asked enough questions without this. She needs rest. On top of that she should have a lawyer present.'

'Mr Phillips,' Henry spoke patiently, as if addressing a slightly retarded child, 'I don't know what you are thinking but you will see there are no witnesses present and I am trying to get to the bottom of a murder. I merely want to know something about the girl's background and, if possible, to find who her friends were. I just want information.'

'And in the meantime there's a crowd outside and goodness knows what rumours are going around. That blasted housekeeper next door has been at it. I saw a reporter come out of there.'

'I am sorry about that but I don't think Miss Smith will bear me any ill will for something I cannot help. The more information I can gather the more quickly we will find the murderer.' His voice was so quiet, so controlled that Roger sat down and felt rather silly and self-conscious.

'I'm sorry but this sort of publicity isn't good for Janie.'

'I know but it is hardly my fault. Do you mind giving me the address of your parents, Miss Smith. I shall have to see them. They may be able to tell me something about her friends.'

He went as soon as she gave him the address.

'What on earth made you get so mad, Roger? He was only asking questions. Actually he was rather nice.'

'I suppose so.' He wanted to say, 'I was mad because I know the damn awful position you are in better than you do yourself. I know what people are going to say and before you can look round your reputation will be torn to shreds and I can't bear it because I love you.'

'You look worn out, monkey face. I'll get Fanny to make us a nice cuppa.' He stood up and then sat down again remembering what Fanny had told him about that Mrs Simmons. The snide hints she had dropped about the association between him and Janie. How surprised she was to see him leaving the house one morning at four o'clock! He knew

Janie didn't care tuppence about the things that might be said but just now she could do without that sort of talk.

'Janie,' the words came slowly because he was hunting for the right ones. 'Janie, don't think I am out of my mind but you know I am terribly fond of you. More than that, I love you. Will you marry me, Janie, and let me take care of all this for you?' He made no attempt to touch her, just looked at her with troubled eyes. Her green eyes were more tender than he had ever seen them and his spirits rose.

'Roger, you are a darling and I love you for all your kindness and help over the years but I can't marry you. I don't think I shall ever want to get married but I am most deeply grateful. I think you are the finest friend anyone could possibly have.'

'Dear little monkey face, I know you don't love me but please, for the time being, let me tell people we are going to be married. I don't want to hold you to any promise but it would make things easier. I could do more for you until after this mess is cleared up.'

'Roger, you are a pet but there is nothing for you to worry over. I'm sure that inspector will have it sorted out before long. He's got the most lovely, determined jaw and I know it will be all right. You were silly to get it into your head that he suspected me. You did, you know. That's why you lost your temper.' She was so confoundedly admiring of that great, ugly flatfoot! Roger was furiously jealous.

'I told him I was in my dressing room when Ted knocked and I looked at my watch and it was half past eleven and I had about three-quarters of an hour before I needed to get ready and I didn't want to speak to anyone. Apparently Ted said that was about the time he knocked and I wouldn't have known if I hadn't been there.'

The silly girl was so trusting. Convinced the man believed her. He probably thought Ted had rung her up and told her what time he knocked! Roger was past trusting anyone. He only wanted to save Janie from nasty, dirty slander. He thought of that family of hers being drawn back into her life and shuddered. If only she would let him take care of her. He knew now how much he loved her. To him it was nothing short of a miracle that anyone should have had the childhood she had and remain so unspoiled. But then, Janie was so utterly different from anyone else. His love was growing to such an extent that he wondered how on earth he hadn't realised before how much she meant to him.

Henry Mason didn't have to go to Lilac Grove. When he got back to The Yard he was told there was a man waiting to see him. Tom Craddock, Celia's father, was sitting in Henry's office. Sergeant Halliday was also there. Tom Craddock didn't get up and Henry immediately took an aversion to him. The bloated face, the big, hairy hands and dirty fingernails, the loose mouth, the strong, yellow teeth and greying, untidy hair. He could well understand why Janie had been taken into care. He didn't remember when he had seen a nastier piece of work.

'Wot I want to know is why I wasn't told of me poor girl's murder before I seen it in the papers. Nice shock it was to me poor wife.'

'If you had been taking more interest in your daughter for the last three months you might have heard of it sooner. As it was Miss Smith was too shocked last night to say much at all and we thought the girl was an orphan.' He lied valiantly, knowing it was an awful slipup on the part of Price.

'That filthy little bastard, taking the girl away from 'er parents. It's a pity they don't 'ang 'em any more or she'd swing.'

'Are you inferring that Miss Smith killed your daughter?'

''Oo else, I'd like to know? It said in the papers that no one broke in. She'd do it all right. If ever there's a vicious little bitch it's 'er. She was only fourteen w'en she attacked me and 'ad to be put under control.'

'Mr. Craddock,' Henry laid great emphasis on the 'Mister', 'if I were you I would watch my tongue. There is a law of slander and I can assure you that no suspicion whatsoever rests on Miss Smith. She was nowhere near the house when your daughter was murdered.' He stared straight into Craddock's pale grey eyes and the man looked back unblinking. 'What is more your stepdaughter was not put under control but taken into care, which is another thing altogether.' He knew he was risking a great deal because he did not know all the facts but he was a shrewd judge and a good guesser and he was certain Janie Smith had had a pretty awful childhood.

'You can call it w'at you bloody well like. That bitch told the p'lice a lot of . . .' He paused and Henry knew he had decided he had better moderate his language. '. . . lies about me,' he finished.

'Have you identified your daughter's body?'

'Yes, I 'ave, poor little bint. Lovely girl she was, too, and goin' to make a fortune until that bastard got 'old of 'er.'

71

'Are you again referring to Miss Smith because if so you have said enough. Now do you mind answering a few questions?'

'Me! Wot for? I'm the one wot wants to know about it. That's wot I come 'ere for.'

'Where were you between eleven and twelve last night?'

There was sudden alarm in the pale eyes.

'I was with a mate if you wants to know. 'Arry Perkins, lives next door to me. Nice thing w'en a man's daughter gets killed and all 'e gets from the p'lice is questions.'

'Your daughter was not much more than a child but although she's been away from home for three months you haven't shown a great deal of interest until now.'

'Precious long three months. She left 'ome last November.'

'Are you sure of that?'

'Course I'm sure. Didn't even leave a note. Just walked out.'

'And you never bothered to find out where she was. Now you are trying to tell me you are upset and that Miss Smith took her away from her parents. She was with her sister for only three months. You had better watch your tongue in future. You are sure it was in November she left?'

'You ask the woman downstairs. She knows.'

'What about your daughter's friends?'

'I don't know. She went around a bit with Lily Jacks down the road and Rita Barrett round the corner.'

Sergeant Halliday took down their names and addresses.

'Now, Mr. Craddock,' Henry was taking a delight in emphasising the 'Mister'. 'I must warn you that if you give any information to the press about your opinion of Miss Smith you will be liable for defamation of character. I should be careful if I were you.'

Now there was something approaching fear in the pale eyes and Henry knew he was too late. Janie Smith was in for a tough time and a lot of mud. He knew it was possible for her to be guilty, she could have left the club and gone to Hampstead and back just as she had on that other night. The fact that she knew the time Baynes knocked on her door only meant that he could have rung her up and told her. But, guilty or not guilty, Henry hated mud slinging by the press—or anyone else for that matter.

Tom Craddock went with his shoulders back defiantly and a quick, catlike walk. For such a heavy man he was surprisingly light on his feet. Henry lit a cigarette and looked at Halliday.

'That's a nasty piece of work if I ever saw

73

one. Boozer, what about a cup of tea?' He grinned, knowing that Halliday could drink tea at any time. 'And we'd better think out a plan of campaign. I want the whole of Miss Smith's past looked into. I don't believe a word that blighter uttered except the bit about when Celia left home but I want details. Get young Hollis on it. He's a bright lad and will go to any lengths to get facts. Then there's Celia Craddock's friends and I want the doctor's report.' Mason picked up a biro and began to doodle. Halliday stifled a moan. The Wonder Boy hadn't a clue or he would be drawing matchmen instead of squares and circles and intersecting lines. He brought back the tea plus the doctor's report. The girl was not a virgin, there was no sign of rape and she wasn't pregnant. The odd thing was that this made him more sorry for Janie Smith. He was certain she would hate this more than anything and somehow they had to find the man with whom the girl had been friendly. He strongly suspected there was more than one. Where had she been during the evening she was killed? The first person he must see was this fellow Neilson. He drank the tea and lit another cigarette.

'Halliday, while Hollis looks into Janie Smith's past you chase up those two girls. They may know something about little

Celia's boy friends. Any rumour about someone with money. I'm thinking of those notes we found. Over a hundred of them. They didn't come out of the blue. Were they payment for services rendered or an attempt to keep her mouth shut?'

* * *

Neville Neilson had a flat in an exclusive block off Knightsbridge and he opened the door himself. It was very elegant and there was an open book of Chopin's sonatas on the beautiful piano. Henry wondered if it was for effect or was he a pianist? Neilson was tall, slim and fair with bright blue eyes, a neat moustache and an easy manner. Henry decided a good public school, university and a good background but this did not mean the man was not a blaggard or even a murderer. He explained the reason for his call and Neilson was the soul of co-operation. He had been shocked when he read of Celia's murder. Henry met charm for charm.

'I understand you considered that Celia Craddock had possibilities and were eager to give her a chance.'

'I still think of her as Celia Smith. She never told me her name was Craddock. She had possibilities and was far better looking than her sister.'

'Funny, her sister and her accompanist didn't think much of her chances.'

Neilson looked at Henry carefully and Henry knew he was debating whether to tell the truth, the whole truth and nothing but the truth or whether this was an occasion when it was better to lie and make it convincing. Whether the lie would be to save his skin or his reputation was another thing.

'Janie Smith and her accompanist were right in one way. Celia could never have been another Janie. She had possibilities and I did think I could do something with her. I'm not a fool and I don't often make a mistake but this time I backed a loser. I hate to admit it but I began to wish I had never seen her.'

'How did you meet her?'

'She went to the Max Twyman Agency and said he had sent her to me.'

'When was that?'

'A couple of months ago.'

'When did you see her last?'

Neilson took a deep breath. 'Last night. She came round here . . .' he paused, 'about eight-thirty and said she had had a dreadful row with her sister about me and her sister had told her to get out. I said she would hardly turn her out at a moment's notice and she had better go back. I drove her home and we reached Miss Smith's house at about nine-thirty.'

'You didn't go in with her?'

'Of course not. I didn't even take the car into the drive.' That Henry believed. Neilson was no fool.

'You didn't notice if anyone was hanging around the house by any chance?'

'Good lord, no. My object was to get her home and as soon as she got out of the car I came back.'

'Did anyone see you come in?'

'I shouldn't think so. I parked the car, came in by the service entrance and spent the rest of the evening reading.'

'What did you think of the girl apart from her possibilities as a singer?'

'Reasonably intelligent, very lovely and at first she pulled the wool over my eyes completely. Later I discovered she was unco-operative and a little bitch. I could have made a singer of her. Not top class but she could have earned a living but she wanted to get there without work. I don't think I've ever known anyone more sure of herself.'

'Did you give her money?'

'A few pounds here and there.'

'Enough to add up to a hundred or so?'

Neilson looked at Henry as if he were clean out of his mind. 'I had known the girl a

77

couple of months, I had told her I would coach her and give her a chance. I had no intention of doing any more until she showed signs of putting in some hard work. If she told anyone I was giving her money like that she was pulling a very fast one.'

'No, she didn't tell anyone that. The money was in her room and Janie Smith says she did not give it to her.'

'She didn't get it from me!'

'Thank you, Mr Neilson, you've been most helpful.'

What he told me was the truth, Henry thought, as he pressed the button of the lift for the ground floor, but I wonder how much he didn't tell me and I wonder if it was eight-thirty when she went to see him?

The foyer was beautifully carpeted and furnished with deep armchairs and settees. There was a small office with a bored looking porter. He eyed the snapshot Henry showed him, shook his head and then suddenly perked up.

'Yes, I have seen her but she didn't look like that. The first time she might have been a schoolgirl but since then she has been more made up and looked years older.'

'Did you see her last night?'

'As a matter of fact I did. Mrs. Hallet-Browne in seventy-two rang down for someone to go up and fix a light. There wasn't anyone else around so I thought I'd go up myself. Probably only a fuse. We're supposed to use the service lift but that's round the back and I didn't want to leave the office for long. The outer door of the lift wasn't quite closed and that girl was inside letting out a string of words because it wouldn't rise. When I said why she gave me a look. Talk about bedroom eyes! Phew!' Then he stopped, realising he had said more than he should. Henry grinned.

'What time was that?'

'Just after six.'

'Are you sure?'

'I don't come on duty until six this week and I hadn't been on more than a few minutes. Full of herself, she was. Said she was going into show business and Mr. Neilson was her manager.' He stopped. 'Good God, is that the girl who was murdered?'

'Yes, but I'd rather you kept this information to yourself.'

'Don't worry, sir, I don't want to get into the papers. The owners of this block wouldn't be too pleased.'

So, thought Henry as he got into his car, you were a little too smart, Mr. Neilson. If the rest of your story was true why lie about the time Celia arrived? and you haven't any alibi at all. As he started the engine he saw a vaguely familiar figure on the other side of the road. He would have recognised that catlike walk anywhere. Tom Craddock by all that was wonderful. Now what was he doing in this district? It was unfortunate that Craddock looked across just then and Henry was sure he recognised him. Wherever he was intending to go Henry was certain he wouldn't go there now! Not with Henry around.

CHAPTER FOUR

It had been a long day and Henry was tired. He went home to the small house in Chelsea which he had recently bought. If anything important cropped up at The Yard they'd phone. He would ring up Beth. It was Mrs. Murdock's evening for visiting her daughter but she would have left his dinner ready. Thank goodness Mrs. Murdock thoroughly approved of Beth and was going to stay on after they were married. He wasn't going to have Beth giving up her work. It had been her life for too long.

The light was on in the living room and the curtains drawn. It was later than he thought. Mrs. Murdock must be back already. As soon as he opened the living room door he saw the difference. The furniture had been moved slightly and, drawn up to the fireplace was an armchair he had not seen before. Deep and comfortable and upholstered in dark blue brocade with just a touch of old gold which matched the carpet to perfection. In front of it was a footstool with the same upholstery. He stared at it with childish pleasure. No need to ask who had chosen them. He sat down and solemnly took off his shoes and put

81

his feet on the stool, leaning back luxuriously and wriggling his toes. Darling Beth, she had an aptitude for choosing comfort and beauty at the same time.

'Like it?' He had been so absorbed in his new possession he hadn't even heard the door open. He was out of the chair in a moment and padding across the room to take her in his arms.

'Perfect for a tired man, my darling. Where on earth did you run it to earth?'

'In a junk shop off the Portobello Road and then I had it and the stool recovered. Go and sit down. Dinner's nearly ready. I knew it was Mrs. Murdock's night out and I told her I would cook.'

He chuckled, his weariness dropping away. 'I believe you feel guilty for postponing the wedding and are trying to get round me.'

'How did you guess?'

They hadn't quite finished their dinner when the phone went. It was Halliday. He had seen the two girls and they both told the same story. Celia had been friendly with a crowd but particularly with a Barry Draper. When Halliday saw him he could give no account of his movements at the time of the murder. Halliday had brought him in in order to 'help them in their inquiries'. He was sullen and would say nothing. Henry wondered if it was the same boy who was in Janie Smith's house. There was only one way to find that out. Beth grinned.

'Don't worry about me, love, I've got to get used to it. Drop me at the nearest tube station. I didn't bring my car.'

'I'll do better than that. I've got to go to Hampstead so I'll run you home first.'

Janie answered the phone and said she would be ready when he called for her. He knew perfectly well she could have gone to The Yard on her own but he wanted to talk to her, to get to know her better. It was tempting to ask Beth to come with him but apart from regulations (which seldom worried Henry!) he couldn't drag her into it.

'You are the most understanding woman a copper was ever fortunate enough to capture.' He held her close for a moment. 'I don't know what I've done to deserve you.'

'Wait until we're married and you'll learn.' Her head was against his shoulder. 'Henry, do you think that girl killed her sister?'

'No, sweetie, I don't, but unless I can clear this case up quickly there's going to be a lot of mud slung.'

'Poor girl, I'm so sorry. To think it was only Saturday when we saw her at The Purple Pelican. She looks as fragile as a piece of porcelain but her voice was so warm and full of

83

feeling.'

'I know and I think she's had a pretty raw deal all her life.'

Janie was wearing a blue woollen coat over a matching dress and hardly any make-up. She looked anything but a nightclub singer. Much more like somebody's confidential secretary. Her smile was friendly but the lost look was in her eyes.

'It's kind of you to fetch me. I could have driven over myself.'

'It's rather late and I thought you might not feel like driving.'

'I didn't. There's been reporters and cameramen outside all day but they seem to have gone now.'

She was mistaken. As they came down the steps a couple of men came round the side of the house.

'Anything to report, sir?' There was a flash of light and Janie shook her head and blinked.

'Nothing at all.' Henry was furious. Why hadn't he walked round the house before he knocked?

★   ★   ★

The boy was sitting in a small room. His jean-clad legs were stretched out in front of him and the chair tipped right back. Long hair hung round his shoulders and the smoke from a cigarette curled up from his fingers. His whole attitude was careless defiance. As Janie followed Henry into the room his mouth curved up in a sarcastic grin.

'It's the boy I saw in my house, Inspector.'

'So what?' He made no attempt to deny it and his expression as he looked at Janie was sheer insolence. 'That's no reason for the bloody coppers to drag me here.'

Henry took Janie to his own office. 'It's a pity I brought you here, Miss Smith, but at first he denied having seen Celia since she left her parents. If you wait here I'll run you home.' He picked up Hollis's report and put it in his pocket. He could read that later. Then he sent Lloyd for a cup of tea for Janie.

Barry Draper was still sitting with his chair tipped back and had lit another cigarette. Henry sat behind the desk and looked at him without a word. Halliday held his notebook ready. The boy began to fidget.

'All right, I admit I was at that bint's house a couple of months ago but I ain't been there since. Now can I go?'

'No,' said Henry taking out Hollis's notes as if he was willing to sit there all night.

'Struth, what d'you want now?'

'What you were asked in the first place.

85

Where were you last night?'

'That's my business.'

'And ours. All right, take him away. He may be more co-operative in the morning.'

'Blast you coppers for a nosey lot of bastards. I was with a girl at Wapping all night.'

He gave her name and address grudgingly.

'Take him away.'

'Do you mean I can't go 'ome?'

'Not until we've checked up. You lied before and you are probably lying again.'

He wilted a bit but said nothing and he was taken away.

'We can find the girl in the morning, Boozer. It won't hurt him to cool off a bit. Give him time to think up another yarn if the girl won't back him up. I'll give you a lift if you like, Boozer.' Halliday's capacity for drinking one cup of tea after another had earned him the nickname. 'I'm going your way. We'll take Miss Smith along. If I don't get you home soon your wife will be after me.' Halliday had only been married nine months.

Halliday muttered, 'It doesn't matter, sir, she's not there.'

'Something wrong, Boozer?'

'The baby's not due for another four months but it looked as if she was going to lose it so they took her into hospital this morning.'

'Then why in hell didn't you say so? Somebody else could have made those inquiries.'

'It's all right, sir. She's under sedation and I couldn't see her. She's rather bad but before she went into hospital she said I wasn't to worry. I'm better working.'

Oh, lord, Boozer hadn't said a word. Not a complaint about the hours he put in and that girl in hospital. Not that she would grumble. He knew her. Pity the public didn't know a little more about the life of a policeman's wife. They might be a bit more helpful.

'All right, Boozer, but go and see her first thing in the morning if they'll let you and thank her from me for being a marvellous woman.'

'I'll do that.'

Henry remembered the wedding. Gillian looking little more than a child in her bridal white. God keep her safe, he thought. Poor old Boozer! He must be worried sick.

Janie went up the steps of her house with Henry by her side. This time there was no one hanging around and she breathed a sigh of relief.

'Good-night, Inspector, and thank you for being so kind.' She got out her key but she need not have bothered. Roger opened the door. He was looking furious but he said nothing. Henry murmured good-night and went. Roger closed the door and Janie went into the small lounge.

'I hardly ever used this room but now it feels so much more cosy than the studio.'

Her shoulders drooped and there were dark circles under her eyes which was hardly surprising as she had had practically no sleep for thirty-six hours. Roger's anger evaporated. That man was a blasted nuisance!

'What on earth were you doing with that flatfoot?'

'I might just as well ask you what you are doing here at this time of night.'

'I rang up to see how you were feeling and Fanny said that damn copper had fetched you. I came round and told Fanny to go to bed and I'd get you some tea as soon as you came in. She looked tired. What did he want?'

'They've a boy in for questioning and they wanted to know if it was the one who was here with Celia.'

'And was it?' She nodded. 'Do they think he killed her?'

'I don't know. He's a nasty, belligerent youngster but I don't suppose he was the only one Celia knew. He just happened to come here.'

'Why on earth did that inspector fetch you? I could have taken you and brought you home if you had given me a ring.' He was seething with ridiculous jealousy. In such a short time she seemed almost friendly with the man. Not only that she seemed to trust him and usually she was on the defensive.

'I think he's kind. I was glad, too, because as we went down the steps a reporter and a photographer came round the side and got a picture of me.'

'With that man! People will think he was arresting you!'

'Don't be silly, Roger. No doubt a lot of people think I killed Celia. What difference will a picture make? And, Roger, I think it would be better if you didn't come here so much just now. After this it is doubtful if I will go back to singing.'

'What on earth are you talking about? You must be out of your mind. Once this is over it will soon be forgotten.'

'Will it? I've a feeling that if the press get hold of Tom Craddock the whole of my background will be plastered over the Sunday newspapers. Can't you see it?' Bitterness crept into her voice. 'I was silly enough to think I could make a good life for myself and I might have done if I hadn't been such a fool. You were right in one thing. I should never have had anything to do with the family once I began to get on.'

'For heaven's sake don't start recriminating. If you hadn't I've a feeling they might have found you and told the world. You only did what you thought was right.' She looked so damnably hopeless.

'And where has that got me?'

'It isn't where it has got you but where you are going that matters. It is a nine days' wonder and after the American tour it will all be in the past.'

'Will it? I sometimes wish I had never left the Johnsons. None of this would have happened then. The year I had with them was the happiest I had ever known. It was a real home with love and kindness all round. If only I hadn't been such a fool as to start singing with the group.'

'But, Janie, you love singing. You've always said so.'

'Singing for the sake of singing, not to get into a rat race. I didn't want to be known, not as I am now, just to sing for my living and Frank and Charlotte thought it was the right thing for me. It would have been if I'd come from an ordinary home. I would have had parents to spend my time with instead of being alone.'

It was too much. Roger, remembering his

own happy childhood, looked down at her and longed to give her comfort and re-assurance. He bent down and took her hands in his, not realising it was the wrong time.

'Janie, don't you know how much I love you and want to take care of you. If you don't want to sing again it doesn't matter. I do earn enough to take care of you you know. I could teach if you don't want me to play at night. We could live quietly if that is the life you want. I love you, Janie.' He pulled her gently to her feet and she was almost in his arms when she pulled away and looked at him with something close to repulsion.

'Marry you! That is the last thing I want to do.' She didn't say. 'It's not you but the thought of any man's arms and lips which fill me with loathing,' and Roger thought she just meant him.

He turned away, what little self-esteem he had was stripped from him, like a young tree stripped of its bark, leaving it tender and shrinking.

'I'm sorry,' he muttered, 'I didn't know you felt like that,' If he had added, 'about me,' she might have understood. 'I'll be going. I take it you would rather I didn't come round tomorrow.'

'Not tomorrow, Roger.'

But when he had gone she wished he had

stayed a little longer. The house was so quiet. She went up to bed but it was impossible to sleep. The past had caught up with her and there was no escape. In the morning Fanny was shocked at the dark circles under her eyes and the weary droop to her mouth.

'You'd better have some breakfast in bed.'

'No, Fanny, I'd rather get up. I'll have a rest this afternoon. If only they could find out who killed Celia.'

'Give the police a little time, dearie. It was only the night before last.'

'It seems much longer than that.'

'Time always crawls when there's something wrong. I'll go and turn on your bath and by the time you've had it breakfast will be ready.'

This morning there were no reporters or photographers in evidence but the thought of the long day ahead hung over Janie like a black cloud. She was used to having the days filled to the last minute. Why had she been so adamant with Roger? They could have run through a few songs although she felt the notes would come out cracked and tuneless. But where would be the sense of practising? Everything she had been working for had suddenly slipped out of her grasp and she was lost and alone. Such a short time ago she had made up her mind to get right to the top.

Now it looked as if she was finished.

She had just finished her bath when Charlotte Johnson rang. They had only heard the news that morning because they never had an evening paper. They wanted Janie to go out to them straight away. She explained that the police seemed to be eternally coming to ask her questions and perhaps it would be better to wait a few days. She would come as soon as it was possible. The sound of Charlotte's voice gave her fresh courage. While they were there she wasn't really alone.

Questions! She was sure the answers were in Lilac Grove. Why shouldn't she go and ask a few questions herself? She knew what Roger would say to that but he wasn't coming round and she couldn't possibly make things any worse.

She put on the blue dress and coat. It was plain and unimpressive. She pulled a small, matching hat over her fair hair. Fanny looked at her anxiously.

'There's nobody about, Fanny, and I must go out for a bit or I shall crawl up the wall.' Her smile was reassuring and Fanny said no more. Perhaps she was wise to go out for a while.

She parked the car well away from Lilac Grove. The area was even more run down than on her previous visit. Lilacs! Were there ever lilacs here? She hoped her stepfather was at work. Her hopes were not realised. He was slumped in a brokendown armchair, his braces dangling over his hips and his stomach bulging over the top of his trousers. It was the first time she had seen him in all those years and he was more repulsive than ever. Her mother was at the sink making a half-hearted attempt to do some washing. The table was piled with dirty crockery. The room smelt of fish and chips, stale beer and tobacco. An empty gin bottle stood by the sink.

'Wot the 'ell do you want?' Tom Craddock glared at her. 'Thought the coppers would 'ave caught up with you by now.'

Janie managed to keep her temper in check. 'There is nothing for them to catch up with. I am as eager to find out who killed Celia as they are. What I want to know is did she come and see you at all during the time she was living with me?'

'Come and see us once you 'ad your 'ands on 'er! Suppose you intended to make a nice little bit out of 'er until you found she wouldn't play.'

'The only reason I had Celia with me was to give her a chance to make something of her life. She had none here.' Her stomach was revolted by the fusty smell, her heart fluttered painfully when she looked at Tom Craddock's loose, red lips. She had not realised how much power he could still have to fill her with loathing, anger and, deep down, a sick terror. Her hands grew clammy and it was as much as she could do to keep her knees steady. Why on earth had she come? What did she think she could learn that the police couldn't? Her mother had left the washing and was sitting on a kitchen chair. She had put on weight and her breasts sagged on to her protruding stomach. The golden hair was in need of a wash but the eyes were still as blue as Celia's, the nose as delicately shaped. Under the different circumstances she could have still been a beautiful woman and the thought made Janie feel even more sick. A ghastly caricature of Celia. What a horrible waste!

'What did you come for?' The look in her mother's eyes startled her. It was neither resentful nor spiteful but frightened and almost pleading. 'Celia 'asn't been back 'ere and that's the Gospel truth.'

'You always was a nasty little bitch.' Tom Craddock scratched his bulging stomach. 'All that trouble you stirred up.'

Fear slipped away and furious anger took its place. Janie in a rage never counted the cost.

'Me stir up trouble! It wasn't me, it was you, you filthy brute, trying to maul me!' She turned to her mother. 'Did you know Celia came to me crying and said he'd tried to do the same thing to her, his own daughter! I may be a bastard but thank God for that. Do you think I want to have any of his blood in me? What's more I may be a nasty little bitch but you haven't refused to take the money I sent to you each month, have you? And what good has it done? Whatever you had you'd be pigs in a sty. I suppose it's gin now instead of beer. You've had the last you'll get from me. You can stay in your midden and rot for all I care.'

They gaped at her and Tom Craddock's face turned an ugly red.

'You'd better be careful wot you say, my girl, I can make things 'ot for you. You and your dirty little mind.'

Janie had been in too big a rage to hear the door open but as she turned to go she saw the way was blocked by a tall, dark man in his late twenties. He was flashily dressed in the latest Carnaby Street style but his glossy black hair was well-cut and he was neatly shaved and his brown eyes were lit with amusement.

'Naughty, naughty!' His smile showed gleaming teeth. 'Bad temper seems to run in the family.'

'What's that to do with you and who the hell are you? I shouldn't think this is your usual haunt.' Her eyes blazed.

'You're mistaken. I collect the rents here.'

'Then I hope you get it. It won't be with my help.'

He stood for a moment, laughing at her, then swiftly he stepped to one side and opened the door wide.

'Allow me, Miss Smith.'

She walked by him with her head high, making sure that even her sleeve did not brush him. How did he know who she was? Rent collectors had altered since she left Lilac Grove. She remembered the sleazy individual who had called when she was there. A skinny man with sunken cheeks, tobacco stains on his grubby fingers, a greasy trilby (which he never removed) on the back of his head and a check suit which hung loosely, as if made for a man twice his size. He was rude and unpleasant but far less objectionable than the present one. She hated the slick, smart Alec type. Funny how clearly she remembered so many people from her childhood. Was it because she had had so little else? Odd, too, how that rent collector reminded her of someone. Someone from a long time ago. It was no use, she could not place him. Not that it mattered.

As she got into her car she noticed there was a dent on the bonnet that hadn't been there before. Not a bad dent but enough to spoil its smooth beauty. Since she had left Lilac Grove she had developed a passion for perfection, a tiny chip on a piece of china ruined it in her eyes. Perhaps it was a trait from her unknown father or a defence mechanism against the filth and misery of her childhood. Well, now there was a dent on her car to remind her of it and of what a fool she had been to try and find out anything about Celia. All she had found out was that Celia had not been back to her parents and much help that was.

Roger was waiting for her when she reached home and with him Inspector Mason. What on earth could he want now? Fear caught at her. Did he suspect her after all? Was he just playing with her like a cat with a mouse? It was the first time she had really thought this possible and the fear looked out of her eyes. Roger was angry. Henry stood up as she went into the studio.

'I'm sorry to bother you again, Miss Smith, but we've discovered something odd. Actually it was yesterday and I should have asked you about it last night but I let it slip out of my mind. The police are not infallible.'

His smile looked frank enough but she did not know if she believed him. What did he really want? She went over to the piano and leant against it then, like a child remembering her manners said, 'Do sit down, Inspector.'

'After you,' he answered and obediently she walked to a chair. Roger sat on the stool.

'What is it now? I've told you everything I know.'

And I wish to the lord we had some proof you were really in that dressing room all the time you said you were, Henry thought.

'In the first place the boy we are holding was definitely at Wapping on the night your sister was killed but not with a girl. She denied it at once. But he was there, breaking into a café. We think there was someone else with him but he won't give whoever it was away. As soon as he knew he might be held on a murder charge he owned up. Not that it would have made any difference if he hadn't. He is one of those youngsters who thinks himself very smart but is really rather stupid. He's left his fingerprints all over the place. But that's not why I am here. You say your sister had been living with you for three months. Do you know where she was before that?'

'Working in a factory and living at home.

At least, that is what she told me.'

'She left the factory last November and she left home at the same time.' Henry stubbed out his cigarette. 'How was she dressed when she came to you?'

'Just the sort of things you would expect a girl to wear who had been brought up in that district and was earning a bit of money for herself. She didn't have much with her and what she did have was flashy.'

'So you bought her clothes?'

'Yes, but she didn't think much of my taste. Said I made her look like a kid.' There was the flicker of a smile. 'When I was out of the way she borrowed mine. I knew because on several occasions there were marks on them that I had not made and I would send them to the cleaners.'

'She gave you no idea where she had been living?'

'I've told you. She said she had just left home because of her father, that he couldn't keep his hands off her any more than he could off me.'

'Did you believe her?'

'I didn't know what to believe. When she was little she would tell me anything to get her own way but she was such a pretty little thing.' Janie's mouth quivered. 'I didn't have anyone else to be fond of. I wanted to believe her, I wanted to help her, but it wasn't much use.'

'I'd like to know where she was during the first three months after she left home. Craddock says he thought she was with you. Can you give me the date she came to you?'

'I think it was the first Monday in February. Can you remember, Roger?'

'It was the second week. We didn't finish the northern tour until the end of the first.'

'And she left home in November. I'd like to know where she was between then and February. She could have been anywhere.' Henry got to his feet with that slow, easy movement that gave the impression that he had all the time in the world.

'You don't think she was with that boy?'

'I shouldn't think so. I don't imagine your sister would have changed one back street for another. You say what she was wearing was flashy. Expensive flashy or cheap flashy?'

'I never thought about it but I suppose they must have been expensive and very old for a girl of her age.'

'I think that's where you went wrong, Miss Smith. You thought of her as a girl but she hadn't been a girl for a long while. For instance, there was the money. I can't imagine she saved it out of her factory earnings and you say you never gave her more

101

than reasonable pocket money. She did get a few pounds out of Mr. Neilson but nothing like that amount. She must have spent money if it was only on bus fares. If we could find out where she got that money and where she was living we might have the answer to who killed her.'

'Why did she come to me at all if she had all that money? It wasn't that she wanted to be with me.'

'I think the answer to that is simple. She wanted to get into show business and thought you would open the door. When she discovered you wouldn't or couldn't she was determined to get there on her own.'

'It wasn't that I wouldn't.' Janie bit her lip. 'No, that's not true. I wouldn't after I heard her sing. Believe me it wasn't jealousy, Inspector, but her singing was cheap and nasty and made me feel sick. I may sing in a nightclub but I earn my living decently. I didn't want my name coupled with hers.'

Henry believed her after the bits and pieces he had heard.

'What happened to the clothes she came in?'

'I gave them to Fanny for a jumble sale.'

Henry shrugged his shoulders. Not much chance of tracing them. Not that it was likely to make any difference if they could.

When he had gone Janie turned to Roger. 'I don't think you should come here, Roger. You know what they say about mud sticking and this is going to stick to me. Celia said she was going to make the headlines and she has and I think she has managed to finish my career at the same time. There is no sense in letting it finish yours, too. When it is cleared up, if ever it is, I shall sell this house and go away.'

'And what do you think you will do then?'

'I don't know. It is something I shall have to work out but I can get some sort of a job. I'm not exactly helpless.'

But that's what you look at the moment, he thought, helpless and despairing, although it isn't much good saying so.

'Talk sense, Janie. The police are not fools although they can be maddening, particularly that blasted inspector with his eternal questions. Once they've found the murderer it will all be forgotten in a few weeks.'

'*You* talk sense! If I were a typist or something obscure it might be but not for a nightclub singer. Whoever did it the public will still be convinced it was my fault. I took her away from her family and then didn't bother to take care of her.'

He wondered if she was right and then thought of the missing three months.

'No, Janie, they won't, not once the police find out what she was doing during those three months before she came to you. You didn't take her away from her family and someone must have seen her during that time. I wonder where she could have been?'

'Your guess is as good as mine. I didn't believe half she said but I never dreamt that she hadn't come straight from Lilac Grove. She must have been with a man. Roger, give me a cigarette, please.'

He lit it for her and wondered what on earth he could do to help but whatever he offered he knew she would refuse. All he could do was to wait and stand by in the hope that she would turn to him in time.

'I'm playing at the Pelican tonight, Janie. Ted says that Manners drowns Lynn. I came in to tell you I'm off to rehearsal.'

'I'm glad, Roger. There is no sense you being idle just because I have to be.'

No sense in me not earning anything, either, he thought.

Janie closed the door on the studio. She wanted to get out of the house and never come back. The house that had been such a joy now filled her with something close to horror and when Roger had gone it was so quiet, so heavy with silence. She went into the lounge and turned on the radio but that

104

made the brooding atmosphere worse and she switched it off again. If only she knew what to do with her time? Until Celia came back into her life she had always been able to lose herself in a book, now she found herself reading the same paragraph over and over again and still not grasping the sense. There was nothing to do. She tried to work out what she would do when it was all over, for she didn't dare contemplate the fact that the police might never find the murderer. Perhaps she could again get a job as mother's help but who would risk employing someone who might have murdered her sister? If only she were a writer or an artist who could work alone! What a good job Roger was working again. Then, for the first time, she knew how much she was going to miss him. The continual friendship which had gone on for so long, the arguments over numbers and how to put them across, the cups of tea after a show, his occasional bursts of temper when she didn't see eye to eye with him, her irritation when he was going around with Liza Gowers, who had too much money and not enough heart! She was even more furious when he was friendly with Mandy Joyce who, Janie was certain, only wanted him for what she could get out of him. The trouble was that Roger was too kind. The way he had said he loved her and wanted to marry her! She was certain it was because he was full of pity for how things were and might even think he was in love with her. Not that it would make any difference. She would never marry.

The front garden was hidden from the road by a high wall which was one of the reasons why she had taken the house. There was a semi-circular drive with an archway at either end so that she could drive right up to the front steps. At one time there had been iron gates but they had probably been removed during the war when metal was in short supply and nobody had bothered to replace them. She had thought of doing it herself but it would have meant opening and closing them and so she had decided against it. Soon the roses would be full out. She stared out of the window and thought how carefully she had planted them and how idiotically pleased she had been with the results. Old Alf, who came twice a week, had said she had green fingers. Dear Alf and darling Fanny. The thought of parting with them brought tears to her eyes. She wouldn't think about Roger. After all it was a business association more than anything and when he did eventually get married they would have been bound to see less of each other. She wondered what Lynn was like. He had never accompanied anyone else since she had been working regularly and the thought hurt, which was silly. She was finished with show business, she was certain of that now, but she could hardly expect Roger to be. Roger was a born pianist, living for his work. How he had urged and coached her in the early days, sometimes losing his temper at what he said was her lack of feeling for the warmth and texture of a song. Without Roger she would have got nowhere. Was he really a showman? She didn't know. Dear God, in all the years she had worked with him she didn't know if there was another Roger underneath. But did she know herself? She had thought that all she wanted was to be a good singer, to have a home of her own and peace and orderliness in it. Only a few days ago she had thought she wanted to get right to the top. Now she felt she never wanted to see an audience again. She was nothing but a pendulum, swinging back and forth.

Who was her father? It was a long time since she had queried that. Had he been a good man who had fallen for her mother's lovely face and then regretted it bitterly. Did he know he had a daughter living or had he died long ago? Perhaps it was her father in her that made her hate the degradation of the rooms in Lilac Grove? No, that wasn't true for she hadn't hated it until she lived in the home when the cleanliness and ordered existence made her realise how much more pleasant life could be. If her mother had had the same chance she might have been different. It would have made no difference to Celia. She knew now that she might have had her mother's face but she was Tom Craddock's daughter with his dirty mind and sensuous body. She could no longer see Celia alive and vibrant but only as a hideous corpse. An uncontrollable fit of shivering made her pull herself together. Going round in mental circles would do no good. She went out to the kitchen where Fanny was scrubbing the floor. Janie looked at her in astonishment.

'Where's Mrs. Welsh, Fanny?'

'She's not coming any more.' Fanny sat back on her heels and looked up with a grin. 'Good riddance. At least the work will be properly done.'

'Why didn't you tell me, you idiot? I could have been doing some housework instead of going out.' She gave the first natural smile she had given since she found Celia's body. 'I'm an awfully good floor-scrubber if you did but know it.'

It was on the tip of Fanny's tongue to say she didn't need any help but from her own knowledge of life she knew that work could

108

be a panacea.

'Well, there is rather a lot to do. You can either finish this or get on with the cooking.'

'I'll finish that. I need to use up some energy.'

But she didn't even start, for the door bell rang. Fanny was on her feet in a moment.

'I'll go. It might be another of those confounded reporters. I'll say you are out. One white lie won't perjure my immortal soul.' She stripped off a pair of rubber gloves. Fanny was rather proud of her hands. 'Here, put these on. No sense in getting your hands in a mess.'

Janie was still holding them contemplatively when she heard Tom Craddock's voice.

'Don't you tell me she's out. 'Er car's out there and I bet she don't walk nowhere. Get outa the way. I'm going to 'ave a little talk with 'er.'

Janie went into the hall still holding the gloves. 'It's all right, Fanny, I'll talk to him. He's Celia's father. What do you want?'

Fanny closed the front door and stood staring at him, her round face hard with anger.

'Celia's father, am I? At least she 'ad one she knew.'

'And much advantage that must have been!' Fanny nearly exploded.

'It's all right, Fanny, I can cope with him. Now tell me what you want.'

'Tell 'er to get out. I'm not talking with 'er 'ere.'

The thought of being in the same house with him made Janie feel sick but she had to know what he wanted. 'All right, go in there but I don't intend to give you more than five minutes.'

He walked into the studio with that smooth, catlike walk which Henry Mason had spotted so quickly. Janie couldn't take him into her small lounge, that would have been another room sullied by an unclean presence. She closed the door and waited. Tom Craddock looked round. He was no fool and knew a lot of money had gone into this house and money was one thing he always wanted. The girl was a lot better off than he had thought.

'Done yourself a bit of good, you 'ave. Enjoying yerself while me and yer mum don't know where to lay our 'ands on a penny. Now look 'ere, me girl, I know we ain't always got on, you always was an 'ot-tempered little bitch but you do the right thing by yer mum and me and I may be able to get yer outa this bit of trouble.'

'If you think I'm going to pay you for something you know you'd better think again.'

'Now come orf it. You know yer in a tight spot. You may be innercent but 'oo's going to believe yer. I thought she'd bin with you all the time, 'struth I did. Suppose I got a good idea where she's bin?'

'Then you'd better tell the police.'

'I couldn't do that. I got me reasons. No, I tell you and you can tell them.'

'And you want me to pay you for the information?'

'It won't 'urt you to give yer mum and me a 'and.'

'I've been doing that for a long time.'

'Well, I don't deny you've sent us a bit but I ain't bin well enough to work for a long time.'

'Tell that story to someone else. How much do you want?' Janie had no intention of giving him anything but she wanted to know how far he would go.

'Nice little place you got 'ere. Most 'ave cost you a few thou. Not that I want to be 'ard.' He looked round the room appraisingly, at the glossy piano, the deep settee and chairs, the cocktail cabinet. He wondered if it was paid for or if she was up to her ears in debt. He wasn't devoid of common sense. Besides, she might not have too much ready cash. Well, if she hadn't got it she could get

111

it. Commonsense deserted him at the thought of how much he had heard that singers earned.

'Let's say five 'undred now and a bit more when you're working again.'

'You dirty swine, get out! If you think I'd pay you a penny you're out of your tiny mind. Get out before I call the police and tell them you are withholding vital information.'

'Now come 'ere. Don't you start that with me. You ain't got no witness and I'd only tell the cops I come to ask about Celia's funeral. I got my rights and I know it. Don't you go bringing the cops on me or you'll be sorry.'

'Get out!' She moved from the door and stood ramrod straight.

'You'll be sorry, me girl, mark my words.'

Janie didn't care. All she wanted was for him to go. Fanny was standing at the back of the hall. She went and opened the door and banged it after him then went into the studio. Janie was standing where he had left her, her eyes dark with misery and wondering what she should do. Should she ring up the police and tell them Tom Craddock had paid her a visit but what good could it possibly do? He could deny it all and it would only be her word against his!

CHAPTER FIVE

Henry Mason sat at his desk and looked at the paper work staring him in the face and made no attempt to deal with it. Boozer had gone to see his wife and Henry was completely stymied. He had had cases in which there were plenty of suspects and no clues. He had had cases in which there were clues but no immediate suspects. This one didn't have much in the way of either apart from Janie Smith and Neville Neilson. Neither had alibis. Janie Smith could have found out the time Baynes knocked at her door when she went back to the club, if she had killed her sister. Neilson had no alibi at all. Janie Smith admitted she had been in a flaming temper with her sister earlier in the day and that she had said she would like to wring her neck but if everyone who said that sort of thing really committed murder the place would be strewn with bodies. Neilson admitted that he wished he had never taken the girl up at all but that was hardly enough reason for murder unless she was being far more difficult than he let on.

Henry was sure that the answer to Celia's murder was somewhere in those three months between when she had left home and then gone to her sister. Hate or fear? Which had been the reason for the killing? He didn't think it had been love. Celia didn't sound the sort to evoke a great love. If only Janie Smith hadn't got rid of those clothes. They might have held a clue. And who had given her the money? Where, when, why and who? Questions and questions with no answers. He had no doubt that for those three months there had been a man but why had she left him? Just for the chance of getting into show business? There was more to it than that he was sure. Pretty little Celia who had always wanted things her way and usually got them. This time she had wanted too much. Why did she go to Neilson soon after she went to live with Janie? Did she just hear of him casually or had she heard something about him, something he didn't want anyone else to know? Henry began to waste government paper by drawing lines and squares. What had Tom Craddock been doing in the district? Not just walking for the benefit of his health, that was for sure. Did Neilson know him? The best thing was to go and find out.

Henry stood outside the flat and listened to Chopin being played exceptionally well and wondered if it was radio, record player or Neilson. When he rang the bell it stopped

114

and it was again Neilson who opened the door.

'Hope I'm not interrupting your listening.'

'If you mean listening to myself, no, I can play when you've gone. What is it this time?'

So he didn't put the music on the piano for effect!

'You must practise pretty strenuously to play like that.'

'Yes, and all I'll be is a very good amateur. I realised that long ago and gave up the thought of ever playing for anything but my own amusement. I might have made a reasonable accompanist but find it hard to sink myself. I have a habit of following my own inclinations and no soloist likes that!'

Henry knew that over this he was being quite sincere.

'I wondered if I should find you at home. I know you have an office where you run your agency.'

Neilson suddenly grinned. 'I don't spend a great deal of time there. I've a damned good manager and, if you must know, I don't have to earn my living. My father left me well provided for. The agency is more or less a toy although it more than pays for itself.'

I bet it does, thought Henry, and is also a means of meeting pretty girls!

'Do you know Tom Craddock?'

'And who on earth is he?'

'Celia Craddock's father.'

For a moment he looked puzzled, then his brows straightened and he gave a slight smile. 'Oh, Celia Smith. Funny, I can't get it into my head she had another name. No, I don't know him.'

'Are you sure?'

'Of course. Girls who want to get on the stage or into pop music seldom bring their fathers with them. Why do you want to know?'

'Because I saw him when I left here yesterday and this is hardly his type of district.'

'And you thought he might have an assignation with me. Come along, Mr. Mason, or Inspector or whatever you prefer to be called, I haven't the slightest knowledge of the girl's family apart from Janie Smith.' There was nothing truculent in his manner, just unconcern.

'You don't happen to know where she was living before she went to stay with her sister?'

'How the devil should I know? The address she had at the moment was all I needed.'

'I suppose so but it was a thought. You said she was sent to you by Max Twyman. Do you know anything about him?'

'Fat little East Ender who was once on the

116

halls.' Neilson suddenly grinned. 'He's straight and happily married and doesn't handle nightclub singers. Neither does he groom them. His is just an agency and variety is his line. Celia had had no experience. She needed a lot of grooming even if she had been prepared to do as she was told.'

'Mr. Neilson, I should be careful in the future about handling and grooming young girls.' He laid the accent on 'handling and grooming'.

'Don't worry, I will. I honestly thought Celia was older than she was.'

'In spite of the fact that the first time she came here she looked little more than a schoolgirl?'

Neilson looked startled. 'I don't know how you know what she looked like the first time she came here but I didn't see her. I was just left a message that a Celia Smith had been to see me. The woman who looks after my flat wrote a note. I found it when I got in but when the girl came a couple of days later she certainly didn't look like a schoolgirl.'

'What did she look like?'

'A girl in her late teens or early twenties, well dressed, too much eye make-up but full of vitality. I thought I could make another Esme out of her. *She* was pretty hopeless when she came to me but now she's a topliner.'

'I've heard of her. Not quite the Janie Smith class, is she? Don't let your enthusiasm for producing topliners get the better of you, Mr. Neilson. It could lead to difficulties.'

Henry left on that note of warning. Was there any point in seeing Max Twyman? It couldn't do any harm but he was no nearer finding if there was any particular reason for Tom Craddock being in the district the day after Celia's murder. He didn't know why it bothered him so much. It could be just coincidence and yet it nagged at him like a sensitive tooth that didn't really ache, just let him know it was there. That and the money.

Max Twyman was fat and dark and friendly. He looked at Henry's card and grinned.

'Well I never. What've I done?'

Henry grinned back. He liked the type. The office was comfortable but as unpretentious as the man. He took a seat, smoothed back his thick hair and relaxed.

'Nothing I hope. No, I've come to ask if you remember a girl who may have called herself either Celia Smith or Celia Craddock. About three months ago.'

'You mean the girl who was murdered? Yes, I remember her. The sort who would impress herself on most men. She called

118

herself Celia Smith and said she was Janie Smith's sister. Candidly I didn't believe her but afterwards I realised there was a vague likeness.'

'Why didn't you believe her?'

'I can't give you any specific reason but I'm a fairly good judge of character. I've met Janie Smith a couple of times and I've seen her work. Hard to believe those two girls were bred in the same stable. There's something essentially nice about Janie Smith, there was something essentially nasty about the other girl.'

'Can you tell me anything else about her, anything you remember at all? Did she say where she was staying?'

'Said she was staying with a friend but as soon as her sister came back from the tour she was on she would be living with her. Whether I looked what I thought I don't know but she added that she wanted to get into show business but hadn't had much experience. I told her I was only an agent and my clients were experienced. She sat with her legs crossed and did her best to interest me in their shape, which was pretty good. She was wearing a P.V.C. coat lined with fur cloth, a mini-skirt and a blouse with the dip so low it nearly showed her navel.' His dark eyes twinkled. 'I know the girl's been murdered but have you ever seen Janie Smith either during her act or privately?'

'Both.'

'Then try and connect her with a cheap little tart wearing an outfit like that. If they hadn't taken them off the streets you would have seen her walking them.'

'You're blunt.'

'You mean crude!' Twyman grinned.

'What date was this?'

'Half a mo. I'll soon tell you.' He turned up a book. 'Always put every caller down. Here we are. January 15th. You know that girl was crafty and she probably grasped the impression she made on me. My business is legitimate. I don't deal with call-girls.'

'Did you send her to Neville Neilson?'

'I didn't send her anywhere. Just told her I had nothing to offer.'

'She told Neilson you sent her.'

'Did she though. Look at this.' He swung the book round and under January 15th there were several names and comments and among them 'Celia Smith. C.L.T. Sent her packing.' He grinned. 'C.L.T. Cheap little tart. My comment. She could have got hold of Neilson's name from anyone but it wasn't from me.'

'And what about Neilson? Do you know him?'

120

He took out a cigarette case and offered it to Henry. Then he sat and stared into space for a few moments.

'A bachelor with money who likes women, has a knack of grooming them if they have a modicum of talent. He doesn't do any of the business side.'

'In other words he doesn't do much work.'

'Don't get me wrong. He's clever and can groom them. He knows what he's doing and seldom makes a mistake. Take Esme.'

'You take her.' It was Henry's turn to grin. 'Do you think he made a mistake by taking on Celia Smith?'

'Did he though! Then I bet she'd changed her style or she really had some talent. He's no fool.' Twyman stubbed out his cigarette and folded his hands on his capacious stomach. 'I still find it hard to believe she was Janie Smith's sister. A cheap little tart like that.'

'Only half sister and they weren't brought up together. Thank you for giving me a picture of Celia Craddock—that's her real name. She didn't give you her address I suppose.'

'No, I didn't ask her for it.'

So, thought Henry as he got into his car, she had already tried to get into show business before she went to live with her sister

121

and, what was more, had the nerve to say she was going to live with her! She also knew that Janie was away on tour. Crafty was the word for young Celia but she had been too crafty! She had known how to handle her sister but there was one person she hadn't known how to handle. There was no doubt she had changed her style when she went to see Neilson.

Where had she been living during those three months? Somehow that mystery had to be solved. He wished London had a red-light district for he was sure that was where he would have found traces of her. Apart from that visit to Max Twyman the girl seemed to have vanished underground for three solid months. What had she been up to, where had she been? Once Craddock knew she hadn't been with her sister all the time did he suspect where she had been? He'd send Boozer along to see if he could get anything out of him. Boozer was clever at handling his type. A mixture of affability and gentle pressure.

In the meantime he had better get rid of some of that paper work. Thank God the Super was off sick! Fortunately for him his ulcer had caught up with him before he died of apoplexy in one of his bursts of temper! Henry grinned. He hoped the old devil

122

wasn't feeling too bad. For all his irritating way he liked him. This evening Beth and he were going to the pictures. Life might be worse. Thank the lord she liked Westerns as much as he did. So uncomplicated. You knew the bad men from the beginning and he wished he did in real life. There was the inquest in the morning but that was nothing to do with him. Price had that job and he felt sorry for Janie Smith. Poor little devil. Why had she been fool enough to lock herself into her dressing room? He parked the car and suddenly realised he had wiped Janie Smith off as a suspect.

Boozer was looking much more cheerful. His wife was definitely better and they talked about letting her home in a couple of weeks or so, providing she took things very easily. He went off to see if he could get anything out of Craddock.

Beth was looking wonderful in a springlike outfit of her favourite green. Henry told her so.

'Henry, you are a lamb. Most men give their compliments before the woman says "yes". You've only just started.'

'I,' he said, his ordinary face lighting up with mischief, 'am no ordinary man.'

'Big head!'

They were drinking coffee after the

Western when Beth said, 'Henry, I'd like to do a portrait of Janie Smith. Could I ask her or would that be out until this business is over?'

'Why this sudden urge?'

'When we saw her at The Purple Pelican there was a loneliness about her that I haven't often seen. Once I saw it on the face of a child in an orphanage. I went with some friends of mine who were looking for a baby to adopt. This child had a nasty scar on his face and limped badly and he stood against the wall talking to none of the other children. It wasn't so much unhappiness. He smiled cheerfully enough at the woman in charge but the loneliness was there just the same. Thank goodness Mary and Sid saw it, too. They took young Frankie. His mother had given him the scar on his face and his father had pushed him down the stairs and broken his leg. It wasn't until the next beating that it was reported. It wasn't just the scars on his body but the scar on his mind. His body is still scarred but his mind hasn't a blemish, thanks to Sid and Mary. He knows how much he is loved but it took years to convince him. Janie Smith is scarred in the same way. I hope that some day the scars will fade but I'd like to paint her now.' She paused and looked at Henry with something close to horror. 'I have the nastiest mind, to want to catch an expression of loneliness.'

'No, my sweet, I know what you mean. Something which you hope is fleeting but you still want to catch it. Why did you ask me? I don't know what you do in the daytime.'

She knew what he meant. You might also be able to help her but don't tell me anything about it.

'Will you be seeing her tomorrow?'

'I shouldn't think so. It's the inquest on her sister in the morning.'

He took Beth back to her friend and then went home. Mrs. Murdock had left a note by the telephone. 'Sergeant Halliday has rung several times and asked if you would give him a ring at his home.'

Boozer sounded fed right up.

'I can't get hold of Tom Craddock. He hasn't been home since early this afternoon. I tried the local but he didn't put in an appearance and none of his mates had seen him since midday. The barman said he was in a better temper than usual.'

'So he has the reputation for a bad temper.'

'Seems so. I hung around until closing time and then went back to Lilac Grove but he hadn't come home. His wife didn't seem concerned so I suppose this isn't unusual but she was mad because he hadn't given her any money and he had said he would tonight. I've put a man on to find out when he comes back. He's never been inside but the local chaps reckon he should have been. Nothing big. Petty thefts but they've never been able to catch him.'

'O.K., Boozer, he'll probably turn up in the middle of the night and let's hope they catch him with something on him. He's a nasty piece of work.'

But in the morning Tom Craddock had not turned up. No one had seen him. Could he have bolted?

'Boozer, get hold of the man next door to where he was supposed to have been on the night of the murder. Craddock is known to have had a bad temper. Could he have been waiting for the girl when she went back to Hampstead and tried to get money out of her and when she refused lost his temper?'

'His own daughter! And wouldn't he have been the sort to use his hands rather than a scarf?'

'Who knows what anyone will do and he had told his wife he would be home last night. Did he see you and get windy? I don't like it. I've got a nasty feeling.'

Boozer went off to get hold of Harry Perkins and Henry sat at his desk with a beautiful piece of government paper and

126

began to draw his little matchmen. Had Boozer been there he would have been delighted but he would have been wrong. Henry couldn't see daylight at all, he was just trying to make some kind of order out of all the tiny ends which seemed to have no relation to each other. There was Max Twyman. Nothing to do with the case in the strict sense of the word but with a very clear eye for the type of girl he thought Celia was. Not that Henry thought he was wrong. But Henry began to think that Celia could have been another type if it suited her, for a time at least. Neville Neilson's story about only giving her a few pounds. Had he given her far more than he said to buy her off but she refused to be got rid of? He had had plenty of opportunity to kill her but Henry couldn't think the motive was great enough.

Esme was singing at The Matador. Not really his cup of tea and not the place he would want to take Beth. Besides, if he took Beth it might be difficult to get friendly with Esme and that made things complicated. Why had he been silly enough to tell Beth they would have a nice, quiet evening? With a case like this he should have known it was impossible. He began to wish he had a nice, quiet office job from nine-thirty till five-thirty or whatever the usual office hours were. He rang Beth and told her he wouldn't be able to see her and she sounded quite happy about it and that made him even more irritable. Beth accepted the fact that he seldom knew when he would be free far too cheerfully. Anyone would think she didn't want his company. Then he called himself a rude name. He was becoming a perpetual grouser. But he should have been on his honeymoon!

When Harry Perkins arrived he was very subdued. A shifty little man with eyes that never looked at you. He wore an old navy-blue suit and there was dandruff on his collar.

'According to you Craddock spent the whole of Monday evening and half the night playing cards with you. From eight o'clock until two in the morning.'

''Sright!' Perkins stared at the papers on the desk.

'Now why did you tell that pack of lies?'

'It's the truth.'

'It's a pack of lies and you know it.' Henry was chancing his arm and *he* knew it! 'Come along, you'd better own up before you make things worse.'

Perkins shuffled his feet but he didn't speak.

'What's the matter, man? Are you scared of Craddock? If you are then say so. You'll get protection.'

'He's a nasty-tempered blighter.' Perkins shuffled a bit more and sniffed. When he did look at Henry his eyes were wide with fright. ''E told me if I didn't say 'e was with me 'e'd break my arm and 'e would, too.'

'When did he tell you this? Before the girl was murdered or after?'

'The day before. No, not the day before, in the afternoon.'

'Make up your mind.'

'Monday afternoon.'

'Have you ever done anything like this for him before?'

'Once or twice. Look 'ere, guv, don't you tell 'im I let on. 'E'd break my blooming neck.'

'Do you know where he went?'

''Course I don't. Get away from 'is missus 'e said.'

'And I suppose Craddock slipped you something for giving him an alibi?'

'Ten bob now and agen but it wasn't the money, honest it wasn't.' Sweat glistened on the wrinkled forehead. 'Tom's not the sort of bloke you wants to get on the wrong side of.'

'Do you know a boy called Barry Draper?'

'The kid what was friendly with young Celia?'

'Yes. Have you seen him with Craddock?'

129

'Sometimes I see them talking in the local. Just chatting like.'

'All right, you can go and you'd better be careful in future about the yarns you tell.'

He looked as if he would rather stay where he was. Craddock was far more frightening than the police to this man.

'Off you go. We'll keep our eye on Craddock.'

Perkins went, reluctantly.

'Boozer, I wonder if Craddock did that job at the café with Barry Draper?'

'He couldn't have done that and strangle his daughter.'

'I know but why did he arrange an alibi with Perkins on Monday afternoon? Craddock wouldn't plan a murder, it would be done because he lost his temper. But where is he now? I can't imagine him bolting for fear Draper gave him away. Brazen it out more likely.' Henry was drawing. A matchman with his arm round a matchwoman. Halliday wondered in which direction The Wonder Boy's mind was working. He seemed to be skipping from one idea to another but Henry was not given to talking about things.

'Boozer, put young Hollis on to that coffee bar near Lilac Grove. He can look the beatnik type when he puts his mind to it and I want to know if Celia was ever seen with anyone apart from the youngsters who hang around there. Then you can go home.' He suddenly grinned. 'I'm having a night out at the government's expense.'

CHAPTER SIX

Henry had told Beth the inquest wouldn't take long and she was certain Janie Smith would go home immediately after if only to get away from curious eyes. She parked her little runabout in a side road. It was three p.m. Time for the girl to have eaten her lunch and rest for a while. Even now Beth wasn't quite sure of why she wanted to talk to Janie or if it would do any good. She did want to paint her portrait but it wasn't only that. She had a feeling the girl needed a friend and Beth believed in hunches as much as Henry did. Funny that she kept connecting her with young Frankie. He had been given help when he needed it and she could have no more restrained herself from trying to help Janie Smith than fly. How she was going to do it she didn't know. Oh, dear, she did hope Henry wouldn't be mad with her but she was sure he wanted to help the girl as much as she did.

She walked round the drive and up the half a dozen steps to the front door. Beth wasn't the nervous type. When she made up her mind to do a thing she did it. The door was opened by a pleasant, middle-aged woman wearing a nylon overall.

'May I see Miss Smith, please. My name is Fuller. She won't know me but I am here on business.'

The woman eyed her carefully. 'Are you a reporter?'

Beth smiled and when she smiled it was something, lighting her small, round face and making her eyes twinkle. Both Beth and Henry had one thing very much in common. Smiles which lighted up their faces and warmed the hearts of those to whom they were given.

'No, I'm nothing to do with the press and I'm not a writer at all. What's more I have nothing to sell and if I did I wouldn't know how to start door-to-door salesmanship.'

'Then will you tell me what you want? Miss Smith is not too well.'

'As a matter of fact I'm an artist. Mostly I do pottery but lately I've been going back to an old love—portraits. I've seen Miss Smith, I'd like to do a portrait of her and I know she isn't working just now. If I could talk to her perhaps I could persuade her to sit for me.'

'Are you sure there is no other reason?' Fanny was still looking doubtful.

'Nothing unless you count a friendly feeling. Life hasn't been easy for her lately, has it?' Beth paused and suddenly her fair skin flushed fiery red. 'I'm sorry. You must think I have a colossal cheek.'

'Come inside.' As soon as Beth was in the hall Fanny closed the door. 'I think it would be good for her to talk to another woman. She's only got me here and she needs someone, poor child.' She opened the door of the lounge. 'Here's someone to see you, Janie.' Then she muttered, 'Oh, lord, don't you dare let me down.'

Janie was sitting with an open book on her lap but Beth thought it was nothing more than a gesture. An effort to look as if she was unconcerned, probably for the other woman's benefit. Beth gave her warm, friendly smile.

'I hope you'll forgive me for coming at a time like this but that is part of the reason. I'm nothing whatsoever to do with the press but when I saw you at The Purple Pelican I wanted to do a portrait of you. I know how busy you must be normally and I wondered if you would sit for me now you are having a few days' rest. I'll go at once if you would rather.'

It said a lot for Beth that Janie took one look and accepted her. There was the same warmth in her face that had drawn her to Charlotte Johnson. A straightforward simplicity and at that moment Janie was conscious that she needed a friend. Of course there was Fanny but although they loved each other there was little talking point between them.

'Sit down and tell me why you want to do a portrait of me.'

'Because you have much the same expression as a little boy once had. Expressions intrigue me more than looks. I'm Beth Fuller and I've only recently started doing portraits again. I dropped them for pottery. Little figures mainly. I used to have a shop in a picturesque village and sold all kinds of local crafts but I sold it and came back to London.' Beth was talking to give the girl a chance to think. She didn't want to rush her. 'It's nice to be back.' She took out her cigarettes and offered one to Janie who shook her head.

'I don't often smoke. It isn't good for the voice.' She shook her head as if considering, then gave a rueful smile. 'I don't know why I should worry about that now. I doubt if I shall ever go back to singing.'

'That's a defeatist attitude.' Beth spoke briskly. 'You're a natural singer and when this is over of course you will go back. Think of all the pleasure you give to other people. Even if you don't go back to the same sort of singing you will have to sing. It would be just as silly for me to say I wouldn't paint or make my little figures again.'

135

'That's different. You can do that without standing in front of an audience. You don't need to be looked at.'

'I know it has its advantages but a natural bent has to be used or part of you would die.'

The door opened and Fanny brought in a teatray. She looked at Janie's face and saw an interest there that she hadn't seen for days and knew she had been right to ask Beth in.

'Bless you, Fanny, we could do with a cup of tea, couldn't we, Miss Fuller?'

'Thank you, I should love one and my friends call me Beth. Actually they used to call me Betty but my fiancé calls me Beth and I like it much more.'

Fanny went back to the kitchen well pleased.

Janie poured the tea and handed a cup to Beth. 'What good angel inspired you to come and see me? I don't think it was just that you wanted to paint my portrait.'

'Not altogether. I'm one of those people who rely on hunches and felt I had to come. A feeling that I might be able to help in some way but I want to do that portrait. As soon as I saw you I knew that. May I do a few brief sketches while you sit and talk or just sit?'

'Tell me a bit about yourself while we have our tea and I will have that cigarette, after all. Do you live near here?'

136

'No, I'm staying with a friend. As a matter of fact I should be on my honeymoon but my only brother broke his leg in Canada just before he should have flown over. I haven't any other near relatives and I did want him at the wedding so it was postponed.' Suddenly she giggled, an almost girlish giggle. 'I never thought I'd get married. When I was young I was terribly choosey and nobody I ever thought I could marry looked at me twice, then I met my fiancé.'

'Is he an artist?'

This was getting dangerous. 'No, but he's very good and doesn't mind that I get crazy spasms of work. He works for the government.' At some time Janie might know about Henry but it was better for all their sakes that she didn't know now.

'I don't think I shall ever marry. I don't really like men. Of course, my accompanist, Roger Phillips, is nice and very kind but he's different.'

Beth didn't ask why he was different but got out her sketch block. The 'alone' look was there and Beth drew some quick, vigorous lines, trying to capture that 'lost' expression.

'Men are all different, just as women are.' Beth spoke casually. 'Some are kind and gentle, some care for no one but themselves.

137

When either sex are like that I think they are to be pitied. They miss so much.'

'You'd feel differently if you knew my stepfather. It isn't that he only cares for himself, he's more like an animal, a sly, nasty wolf with a slimy mouth.' The lost look gave way to one of sheer revulsion. She sat there brooding and suddenly spoke again. 'It's funny but he wasn't at the inquest. I thought he would be if it was only to say something horrible about me.'

'Why should he?'

For years Janie had buried her feelings, refusing to talk about them but Beth's casual manner that yet had so much friendliness and her common-sense attitude opened the floodgates and Janie longed to talk to someone who would understand, just a little.

'My mother had me before he married her and I think he always hated me and he's nasty, right through. He came here yesterday and said he knew something about Celia and wanted me to give him some money for what he knew. Because I wouldn't he said I'd be sorry. I thought he would say something at the inquest but he wasn't even there.'

'Have you told the police?'

'No, there was really nothing to tell.'

'But you should have told them he threatened you. It might help them in some way.'

'But how could it? He'd only say I was telling lies to get him into trouble.'

'I still think it might help. After I've gone why don't you ring up whoever is in charge? It couldn't do any harm.'

'I suppose not.' Janie sat thinking.

Beth was looking at her sketches. Janie's face from different angles. Not strictly a beautiful face but the haunting expression and the soft colouring would make a lovely picture but she had to find the best angle before she started the real portrait.

'You tell them. It's amazing how a little bit of information might help. Like a picture. One little line makes all the difference. May I come tomorrow? Look, this is what I've done but I'm still not sure of the right angle.' Beth handed the sketches to Janie.

'Do I really look like that? It's not like my photographs.'

'Most photographers merely want a lovely picture. I want more than that, the side of you that doesn't always show. May I come tomorrow?'

'Yes, I'd be glad of your company.'

Beth went away satisfied. She hoped to goodness the girl would ring Henry.

Henry was just leaving the office when the phone rang. He swore under his breath. The damn thing was never silent. What was it now?

Janie Smith's voice came over the line, very small and quiet.

'I'm sorry to bother you, Inspector Mason, but I've something I should tell you. I ought to have rung you before.'

Better go and see her. Henry didn't like information over the phone.

Janie was still sitting in the lounge but there was a more hopeful expression on her face and he was sure Beth had been to see her. He felt a sudden pride in the woman of his choice. She had a wonderful trick of bringing comfort and a sense of peace.

'I hope I'm not being a nuisance and that what I have to say may be helpful.' Quietly she explained.

'Haven't you any idea what this information could be?'

'No idea at all. What could he say that would make me sorry? I haven't done anything. It seemed just bluff to get money out of me. I told him to go to the police but he didn't go to the inquest.'

'Miss Smith, I don't think he meant that at all. He may know something that would take any suspicion from you and that is why he said you would be sorry. It's a pity you didn't tell me this at once. It might have made a difference. Why have you told me now?'

'A friend said I should.'

'A wise friend. And he said nothing else, spoke of no one else?'

'No, he just said I would be sorry.'

Henry thought that if Craddock was trying to get money he might be the one to be sorry! As Henry was getting into his car Roger Phillips walked up the drive. If looks could kill Henry would never finish the case! He tried not to smile. Mr. Phillips was on the war path.

Fanny opened the door and Roger didn't even greet her.

'What did that damn policeman want this time?'

'I wouldn't know,' said Fanny, deciding that Roger was behaving like a fool. Just when Janie wanted comforting Roger did just the reverse. She had always thought men were fools but she rather liked that policeman.

'Roger, I told you it would be better if you didn't come here so much.' Janie looked up with troubled eyes. Roger had played such a big part in her life for the last few years and she was going to miss him but the sooner she got used not to seeing him the better. Whatever Beth Fuller said she could never face going back to The Purple Pelican. She could imagine the things people would say. 'You

know she was suspected of killing her sister!'
She had almost given up hope that whoever
did it might be caught.

'I suppose you'd rather see that blasted
policeman!' The anger in Roger's voice startled her. 'What did he want this time?'

'I sent for him.'

'What on earth for?'

'Because my stepfather came here yesterday and I thought he should know.'

It was the first time Roger had heard her
speak of Craddock as her stepfather. It was
almost as if she was deliberately trying to
make him see her real background. As if she
wanted to cut herself off from her present
life.

'Janie, you are behaving like an idiot.
Anyone would think these last years were
nothing at all.'

'They're not, really. I know now that you
can't step out of your background as if it
doesn't exist. It's there and it wouldn't
matter what I did it would always be there.
Like an ogre waiting to pounce. After Celia's
funeral I am going to sell up and go right
away.'

'Don't talk such rot! What about your con-
tracts?'

'I don't think they will matter. Nobody
will want me after this so there won't be any

difficulty.' She knew she was making him even more angry but she didn't care because it was easier to quarrel with Roger than just say goodbye.

He saw the lost look on her face and stopped arguing and wished the police showed more initiative. He was sure they hadn't a clue as to who was the guilty person.

* * *

Henry was feeling far more hopeful but he wished the silly girl had rung him up immediately Craddock had left her house. The first thing to do was to pull him in—if he wasn't already in trouble. Thank goodness he had seen him himself. His own descriptions were always vivid. Henry gave his orders and then went to The Matador.

Esme was a very different kettle of fish from Janie Smith. Come to that The Matador was a whole heap different from The Purple Pelican. So was the clientele. Esme was wearing a blue dress which was cut up the side to show a vast amount of shapely leg as she moved and the bodice was cut so low that a man of less experience than Henry might have blushed. Esme was very obvious. She walked between the tables and the expression in her eyes was an invitation. She gave Henry an amused smile and walked on. He waited until her number was finished and told the waiter he wished to see the manager. The waiter looked nervous but as soon as he saw Henry's card he went without question and a few moments later he was back.

The manager's office was more than comfortable. It was positively sumptuous and the manager almost too friendly.

'Nothing wrong, I hope, Inspector Mason.'

'I hope not, too.' Henry was his most bland. 'I want to have a few words with Esme. I won't keep her long.'

'Would you mind waiting until after her next number? In the meantime what can I offer you?'

No sense in making the man edgy. 'A small whisky would fit the bill nicely.'

Henry took the cigarette he was offered and made his usual remark about smoking too much then leant back in the luxurious armchair and looked as if he had all the time in the world and nothing whatever to worry him.

'Would you like to speak to her here or in her dressing room?'

'Here will do, thank you.'

Esme was full of bonhomie. There was a hint of devilment in her eyes and Henry grinned. He could never judge her type harshly. There was a spirit of comradeship about them and he was always conscious that if it were not for his own sex they would not be what they were.

'So,' she sat on the desk and showed as much leg as possible and Henry knew it was not really for his benefit but force of habit, 'The Wonder Boy himself comes to The Matador. What's cooking?'

'Nothing that need worry you. I want some information about Neville Neilson. I understand he groomed you. I believe that is the right way to put it.'

'What do you want to know?' Esme's grin was expansive. 'Whether he groomed me in exchange for being a sleeping partner?'

'No, I'm not really interested in his morals, or yours come to that!' Henry smiled. Esme had a sense of humour. 'Do you know anything about his association with a girl called Celia?'

'You mean Janie Smith's sister. The one who got herself strangled.'

'That's the one.'

'I haven't seen Neville for two or three months but I heard he'd taken her up. Look, if you've any ideas that he killed her, think again. He's strictly non-violent. Much more likely to get himself killed one of these fine days.'

'What makes you say that? Look, Esme, your name need not come into this. Is he in some sort of racket?'

Her laughter was genuine. 'The only racket he's in is his liking for women. One at a time, though, and when he is tired of them he sends them packing. No, what I meant is that one of these days he'll catch one that won't want to be pushed off then the fat will be in the fire. Mind you, he's honest enough about it. He makes it clear from the start that it is only on a temporary basis and once you are launched and making a living he starts all over again with someone new. Have you got a cigarette?'

When it was lit she swung her legs and looked quite serious.

'He never takes a girl on who won't be able to earn her own living given the chance but I've heard rumours about little Celia. Not only was she younger than he thought but she'd been around more than he thought and don't ask me where I got the information because I'm not telling.'

'Any more than you are likely to tell me who had the nerve to speak to you of me as The Wonder Boy!'

'Not on your sweet life. I know when to keep my trap shut!'

'And that's all you know of Neville Neilson?'

'Apart from a few intimate details which I'm sure you don't want.'

'No, spare me those.'

'He's a good pianist.'

'I gathered that myself.'

'Then our interview is at an end. Pity, I was just beginning to enjoy it.' Her grin was infectious. He wondered what her background was. Almost as if she knew his thoughts she answered them. 'Unlike that poor devil, Janie Smith, Inspector Mason, I come from a good middle-class family. The industrial midlands and the whole lot of them so good and so narrow I kicked over the traces and so far I haven't regretted it. Whether I will in the future is anyone's guess. Heaven preserve me from people who are too good. They send some of us to the devil.'

'How do you know anything of Janie Smith's background?'

'The information followed little Celia.'

For the first time Henry thought he was getting warm.

'Esme, I know you don't want to tell me where you got your information but it may be very important. Stretch a point and tell me.'

'Oh, I don't suppose it will make much dif-

147

ference. It was Monty Frank. Neville's manager. I don't know where he got it from but I don't suppose he'd mind telling you. He's a decent sort and runs the Neilson agency very efficiently.'

'Thank you, Esme. Let's hope this business doesn't ruin Janie Smith's career for her.'

'If she has any sense she'll make publicity out of it. That's what I would do, anyway.'

Henry believed her. Nothing would keep Esme down. It was odd but she could have been far more a product of an East End slum than Janie and yet he believed everything she had said. There was an amusing honesty about her.

When he arrived at The Yard the following morning he was told that nobody had seen or heard anything of Tom Craddock. Henry was getting nervous. He didn't like it at all. Young Draper still refused to say who had been in the café robbery with him and when the officer in charge asked if it was Craddock he laughed in his face.

'You're off your rocker,' was all he said.

It did seem far-fetched for a man of Craddock's age to work with a raw youngster but where had he been and why did he want an alibi for that evening? That he was capable of murdering Celia Henry had no doubt but if he had why go to see Janie? Or was he trying to get money out of her on a bluff in order to get away? No, far more likely he did know something and had tried to get money from someone else having failed with Janie. Where was he now? Whatever Esme said about Neilson it was odd that Craddock had been in his district so soon after the murder.

A couple of hours later Boozer came in with Old Joe. He was a wizened scrap of humanity with scanty hair, hardly any teeth and his face yellow and wrinkled with a life spent mooching about the slums picking up odd bits of information and odd shillings doing any job that happened his way. Nobody took much notice of Old Joe. He sank into his background as easily as a hot knife slips into butter.

He sat down on the other side of Henry's desk and his watery eyes stared at Henry mournfully.

'That chap Craddock,' he said without any preamble. 'He got into a dark grey Jag on Tuesday. Late afternoon. Along the Whitechapel Road. Don't know the number of the car. Didn't see him myself but the chap who did isn't likely to come and tell you.'

'Sure it was a Jaguar.'

'Pretty sure and I'll tell you this. It wasn't a casual pick-up. He was waiting for the car.

Not that anyone with a Jag would be likely to offer him a lift.'

'O.K., Joe, it may help but I wish the chap had seen the number. There's a lot of grey Jags about even if the country is going through an economical crisis—when wasn't it?'

Joe went as casually as he had come.

'Boozer, find out what car Neville Neilson has and as soon as you can. And for the Lord Harry's sake be discreet. Could I be very much mistaken in that man? What's more we'll post Craddock as missing. We've got to find him and as soon as possible. Has Hollis any more information about Celia's friends yet? I've a feeling that coffee bar didn't know a great deal about her movements though.'

He was right in one way but Hollis came up with some new information none the more for that. Hollis, with his dark hair combed forward over his forehead, a black leather jacket and tight jeans looked anything but a copper and Henry gave an inward smile. He had been right when he first met the lad on the Wellington Burgess case [*Follow My Leader* (Hurst & Blackett)]. He had as big an aptitude for sinking into his surroundings as Old Joe.

'Before she left home she used to sometimes disappear for a day or so but nobody

150

seems to know where she went. The general opinion is that there was a man in it because she was never short of money. Finally she got the sack from the factory for taking days off.'

'So she was never short of money even before she left home. Interesting.'

'But nobody has a clue where she went after she left Lilac Grove for good although one girl says she went up to Oxford Street one day in January and saw Celia in a big grey car. She didn't know what make of car, only that it was a big grey one. Neither did she see who Celia was with because the traffic was moving for once and she was too surprised to see her to notice who was driving. From the way she spoke Celia was out to trade with anyone who had money. Said she tried it on with the chap who collects the rents round there but he turned her down. I said I supposed he'd got a big car, too. The kid laughed and said he had a little red car and she thought it was an Anglia but she didn't know much about cars, only motor bikes.'

'And that was before Celia went to stay with her sister. Quite a girl where the men were concerned. Too smart for her own good.'

Halliday came in with the interesting news that Neilson had a dark grey Jaguar. Henry stared at him.

'I think I had better make another call on Mr. Neilson.'

Neville Neilson was not playing the piano. He was entertaining a luscious brunette with a voluptuous figure and melting brown eyes. He wasn't put out in the slightest by Henry's visit.

'Run along, sweetie, I'll give you a call.' He beamed at Henry. 'Sit down and make yourself comfortable. I'm beginning to get used to having you around the place. What has happened now?'

He showed no sign of anxiety. If he has a guilty conscience he keeps it well under control, Henry thought.

'I'd like to know if you remember just where you were and what you were doing the day before yesterday. Just the afternoon and evening.'

'That's easy. I drove down to a little village in Sussex. Meadowling to be precise.'

'Any particular reason?'

'There's an antique dealer there and I know he picked up some very nice china at a sale recently and I wanted to have a look at it.'

'What time did you leave?'

'About two-thirty and I got home at about midnight.'

'Did you buy the china?'

152

Neilson grinned. 'No. When I got there the damn place was shut.'

'What did you do then?'

'The same as anyone else would have done. Swore! Then I went to Lewes to some friends and had dinner with them.'

'What time did you get to your friends?'

'Between seven and eight.'

'It took you rather a long time to get to Lewes, didn't it?'

'I didn't hurry. In fact I didn't go straight there. I intended to come home by a round-about route and then altered my mind. I had no reason to come back. What's all this about?'

'Did you give a man a lift?'

'No.'

'Did you go near the Whitechapel Road?'

'Good heavens, no. Why should I?'

No sense in beating about the bush any more. 'Tom Craddock was seen to get into a dark grey Jaguar in the Whitechapel Road late in the afternoon.'

'And although, as far as I know, I've never seen Tom Craddock in my life and there are God above knows how many dark grey Jags about, I must have given him a lift! Why not ask him who gave him a lift?'

'Because we don't know where he is. He hasn't been seen since and we want him.'

At last there was a positive reaction on Neilson's part but it wasn't fear, it was anger, flaming anger.

'Look here, Inspector, I've had about enough of this. You come here asking all sorts of questions about Celia. All right, the girl was murdered and it's your job to find out who did it and I'm willing to help if possible. I'd taken the girl on with the intention of making a singer of her. If you must know, I'd gone to bed with her occasionally, but I didn't murder her, I didn't know her father and if I did why on earth would I want to give him a lift? To ask him not to tell you I was cohabiting with his daughter? Let me tell you this. I wasn't the first man in that girl's life by a long chalk. She'd had more experience than some women twice her age. She was a tramp and how she happened to be Janie Smith's sister is a mystery.'

Neilson paused as if his anger had worn itself out.

'I'm sorry for the outburst but I am beginning to feel sick at the sound of that girl's name. I don't usually talk about the women I have had affairs with. However bad my morals I don't brag about them. You'd better find out the number of the Jaguar her father took a ride in for it wasn't mine.'

'All right, don't get too steamed up. I'm

just a copper with a job to do. Think things out and you will realise you are not in an enviable position. You were the last one to see Celia alive. You told me that on the night of her death she came here about eight-thirty but I know it was just after six. A stupid lie, Mr. Neilson. I could understand it if that was the time she was murdered but we know it wasn't.'

Neilson began to pace the floor then suddenly he stopped and faced Henry.

'All right. A girl has been murdered not so long after you left her. Would you want to say that she came to see you in very passionate mood, you went to bed with her and afterwards she began to make demands? What would you do?'

'She wanted money?'

'Good lord, no! She was sick of her sister and wanted to live with me! I told her that unless she worked she would never get anywhere and as far as I was concerned she could get out and stay out. She said she would tell everyone I knew her age when she first came and I'd be in a mess. At the time I didn't care tuppence but when I knew she had been strangled it didn't look so good particularly as I had taken her home. I had no alibi, I could have killed her. That's the plain, unvarnished truth and it's not very pretty and I know it.'

'Now her father has vanished and the last time he was seen was getting into a dark grey Jaguar! He may turn up before long. Isn't there anyone who might be able to say they saw you miles from the Whitechapel Road round about five o'clock?'

'At five-thirty I was having a cup of tea in a small road house on the A22.'

'Any reason for them to remember you?'

'I shouldn't think so. I didn't pinch the waitress's bottom.' He gave a rueful smile. 'I begin to wish that was one of my bad habits. Unless they remember I hadn't enough change to pay the bill and gave them a five-pound note.'

'Name of the road house?'

'Something ridiculous. I know, The Cock and Kettle and after this I will inquire closely about a girl's parents before I take her up.'

'Not a bad idea,' said Henry and left.

He must check that story about the road house and if it was true, and Henry thought it was, Neilson did not pick up Craddock. Then who did and where was Craddock?

A couple of hours later they knew. A courting couple had found his body hidden in some bushes on Hampstead Heath. The back of his head had been smashed in by a lump of building rubble which was by his side and his body had been moved after death. If only the clot who had seen him get into the car had also seen the number, or even part of it! Dark grey Jaguar indeed. Was it a Jaguar? If they didn't notice the number they might have got the car wrong! Did Janie Smith know anyone who had a big, dark grey car?

And those missing weeks. It seemed insane that a girl could vanish except for a brief glimpse of her in a grey car. Somewhere in that time she had made an enemy and it looked as if Craddock knew who it was.

Henry broke the news about Craddock to Janie's mother partly because he wanted to see her reaction. She wiped her hands on her dirty apron and looked straight through him. For a brief moment there was a likeness to Janie. A look of utter loneliness. Then, before the lids dropped over the blue eyes, he was certain he saw relief. How much of her feigned indifference was fear of Craddock? He wanted to know.

'Why did you never go to see your daughter once she was taken into care?'

Now she looked at him instead of through him.

'It wouldn't 'ave done much good, would it? She was better orf where she was. I didn't want 'er back 'ere, not with 'im. The other kids was 'is.' She sat down suddenly, as if her legs would no longer take the weight of her flabby body. 'It was better 'e thought I 'ated 'er. When she come to see us after she was doing so good I nearly 'ad a fit. Didn't want 'er to come and the money never did me no good, just 'im. I didn't want it, we never did nothing for 'er, poor little bastard.' Tears trickled slowly down her cheeks and he was certain it was a long time since that had happened.

'When 'e married me 'e said 'e would look after 'er as if she was 'is own and I was daft enough to believe 'im. Not that 'e ever cared about them. Never cared about no one. Well, 'e's gorn and I ain't got to worry no more. Young Gary'll be all the better without 'im. If you see Gloria tell 'er I'm sorry.'

'Gloria!'

'Janie, I mean. Never think of 'er as Janie.' She gave the travesty of a smile. 'Thought Gloria was a pretty name, I did, but I was on'y a kid. Seventeen and a month when she was born. I didn't know much then and I don't know much more now. Some folks is like that. We don't never learn nothing.'

Part of the tragedy of the underprivileged, thought Henry, but Janie Smith would be glad to know her mother had thought about her.

'Have you any idea of a man, or men, Celia was friendly with before she went to her sister?'

'Anyone 'oo was willing to pay for 'er. Celia wasn't a fool like me but she was a bit too smart, like 'er father. She'd make up to anyone if they 'ad money. She tried it with Terry Johnson but 'e just laughed at 'er and said if she wasn't careful she'd be in trouble. Young monkey looked 'im straight in the eye and said, "You like to give it to me?" I clipped 'er.'

'Who is Terry Johnson?'

'Father used to keep a junk shop but 'e's bin dead for years. Done well for 'imself, Terry 'as. Never bin too 'ard on me about the rent.'

'He's the rent collector?'

'Owns all this street now and don't live round 'ere no more. Got a posh flat some-where.'

The rent collector who slapped Celia down. More than once it seemed. Could that be for the benefit of others? But he had a red Anglia. On the other hand it would be as well to ask him a few questions. He might know something. Mrs. Craddock did not know where he lived.

It didn't take Henry long to find out and when he did he had rather a shock. Terry Johnson lived not far from Neilson. He cert-ainly had money to live there. Old junk! Men

159

had become millionaires on it. Was Terry Johnson one of them? Interesting. But before he visited him he would have another talk with Janie Smith. He seemed to be spending a great deal of his time in visiting Janie and Neilson. Oh, well, things happened like that sometimes.

CHAPTER SEVEN

Janie was feeling better than she had done since Celia's death and it was mainly because of Beth. She sat near the window in the studio, the sunshine lighting her bright hair, her hands lying easily on her lap. The studio had lost its horror, for Beth's cheerful, understanding personality had taken over. It was odd about Beth. She didn't say a great deal, she wasn't outstanding and yet when she was present there was an atmosphere of peace. Janie couldn't put a finger on what it was but she was deeply and warmly grateful. Beth was painting vigorously but she did not demand utter stillness from her sitter. She wanted to catch the spirit of the girl and without a certain animation that was difficult.

Janie talked. She didn't think she had ever talked so much to anyone before. She didn't realise how much of herself she was letting Beth see. It was wonderful to be able to talk to someone and tell them how muddled you felt over life in general. She didn't think she could ever go back to singing whatever happened. She would feel as if people only wanted to see her because of what had happened to Celia. Perhaps she could help in a children's home. The sort of home where she had been. There she could do some good.

She stopped talking and thought of Roger. It didn't matter what she said he was still continually in and out of the house. His flat was only a couple of streets away so it was easy. She was going to miss him but it was something she must get used to. She was sure he wasn't really in love with her, only sorry enough to think he was. He would soon forget her but the thought of putting him completely out of her life was a pain she had not expected.

There was a ring at the door and they heard Fanny's quick steps in the hall and then Beth heard Henry's voice. She began to collect her things together and hoped Janie didn't notice the flush that rose to her cheeks.

'You've got a visitor. Will this mess be in the way and may I come tomorrow morning?'

Janie looked slightly bewildered at the speed with which Beth moved, slipping off her smock and into her coat as if her life depended on it.

'I'll see you tomorrow, then,' Beth gave a brief nod, a 'Good afternoon,' to Henry and was gone. Henry grinned.

'Your friend seems in a dickens of a hurry or do you think she took an instant dislike to my face?' He spoke louder than usual to make sure Beth heard.

'I don't know why she went so quickly. She's doing a portrait of me.'

'So I see!' Henry looked at the painting and, as always, was struck by Beth's ability to catch more than a likeness. She was so clever! What could she see in anyone as ordinary as he? 'It's going to be a very good portrait.'

'She's very clever, isn't she? What do you want to see me about?'

There wasn't any need to break the news gently about her stepfather and when she heard the expression on her face was a mixture of horror and relief. Then he told her about her mother.

'I thought she hated me, too.'

'No, but there isn't much doubt that she was always afraid for you. She didn't want you to go back at all, for your sake. Things will be better there now Craddock is dead.'

'Thank you for telling me. It helps.'

'I'm sure it does. Do you know Terry Johnson?'

'I know the name and yet I can't remember him.'

'His father used to keep a junk shop down your way but Terry has moved up in the world since then. He owns Lilac Grove and collects the rent himself.'

'I remember. He was at Lilac Grove the

163

other day. I thought I recognised him but you know how it is when you see someone after years. The face is familiar and yet the familiarity is elusive.'

He was struck by the ease of her words. For a girl who had had nothing but an orphanage education of the primary kind she was remarkably lucid. Probably read a great deal. She was looking thoughtful.

'I can remember him as a boy now although he was older than I. I'm not surprised he's made money. Even then he could swop anything and make a profit. You know the type. They swop a few marbles for a cricket ball and the cricket ball for a pair of skates and end up with a bicycle for the cost of a few marbles.'

'I know.' Henry smiled. 'There's a lot of them around.'

'The type to whom making out of other people is the all important thing. A rather nasty boy who could manage to get on the right side of adults. Clever in a way, I suppose. He probably still gets on the right side of people if it suits him. I wonder why I didn't recognise him straight away?'

'Ten years or so and a difference in dress and manner and maybe accent, too, can fool most people, especially if the years are between fifteen and getting on for thirty.'

'I suppose so. I'm sorry I can't tell you any more.'

'Every little helps. It seems your sister tried to be friendly with him but he turned her down.'

'She never mentioned him to me but then she never mentioned anyone she knew.'

'I'll try not to bother you again. I'm glad the portrait looks like being a success.'

As he went out Roger came in and he made no attempt to disguise his feelings.

'Why on earth is that flatfoot always here?'

'He came to tell me my stepfather had been murdered.'

'Good God, why?' Roger stood quite still and then suddenly let out a sigh. 'At least nobody could possibly think you did that!'

'I don't know what anyone thinks. I don't want to know.'

'You're being sorry for yourself when you should be working. I've just come from a rehearsal with Lyn. That girl is useless and I hate playing for her. Besides, I've written a new song for you.'

'I'm not coming back, Roger, ever. I should hate it after this.'

'Then what the hell are you going to do with your life?'

'I don't know yet but I'll think of something.'

'And to think there was a time when I thought you had guts! Scared of a little talk, scared people will look at you!' He was getting angry because there was a shut-in look on her face, as if there was a part of her she had no intention of letting him see and yet why should it make him more angry than in the past? She had always held aloof from him. She had been far warmer with Frank and Charlotte and with Banstead, come to that. And there was this blasted inspector. She seemed to welcome him. What had that damned man got that she didn't mind his questions? What was his attraction? Roger couldn't know that she didn't mind him coming because he didn't seem to think of her as a woman at all—just as someone in a case. He wouldn't have cared so much if she hadn't altered to him but she had. In some indefinable way it was as if she no longer thought of him at all. As if she would rather she didn't see him. In all the time they had known each other she had at least treated him like a friend. And it was since she had met that confounded policeman!

He walked over to the portrait and stared at it. There was a quality of pathos about it already—a lost child looking from a woman's face. His heart missed a beat. It made him angry. It bared her soul and touched his

166

heart. He wanted to put another expression there. Wanted to see the green eyes alight with happiness. Because the portrait hurt him he said the first words he could think of.

'What a damn awful picture!'

'Inspector Mason thought it was good.'

'And what that bloody flatfoot thinks goes, I suppose.'

'I think you are being silly and unreasonable. He has been very kind.'

'And I'm a blasted nuisance!'

'Oh, Roger, you are awkward. I'm tired of the whole thing. I want these inquiries to be all over so I can go right away and start life again one way or another.'

'And you'd rather I got to hell out of it.'

'I didn't say that but at the moment I don't much care. What I do isn't your business.'

'No, it isn't my business. Thanks for reminding me.'

He went without a backward glance and Janie felt her heart almost stand still with pain. They had been close for so long and now she had turned him out of her life. She knew she didn't want him to go but what had she to offer him?

★   ★   ★

Henry went to see Terry Johnson, the man

who could get a bicycle for a few marbles. A man who knew how to make money and had turned the lovely Celia down, or had he? What a man did in front of others he did not always do when there was no one around.

Terry Johnson had just come in. He looked Henry up and down, not so much with insolence as curiosity. He looked at Henry's card and said, 'Come in. What can I do for you?'

Henry's quick eyes took in the flat. Neat, not over luxurious and definitely bachelor. If he had women in his life he kept them out of his living room.

'Sit down. Can I get you a drink?'

'No, thanks. I came to ask you if there is anything you can tell me about Celia Craddock.'

Relief grew on the darkly handsome face. 'Good lord, is that all?'

'What else should it be?'

Johnson let out a gentle whistle. 'I got mixed up in a car crash yesterday. It wasn't my fault. A mad motor cyclist came out of a side road and in trying to avoid him I ran into another car. It didn't save the cyclist completely and there was an almighty pile up. I thought you'd come to say the fool was dead.'

'Bad luck for you. Much damage to your car?'

'A write-off I'm afraid. Bonnet smashed in.

168

Lucky not to be in hospital myself. So was the other motorist. I don't mind telling you it gave me a nasty shaking.'

Henry wondered if he was trying to sidetrack him or was he genuinely worked up about the accident. It would shake anyone but was he making drama out of it? Trying to avoid the subject of Celia, after all! Henry often had a suspicious mind.

'I'm sure it did but I know nothing about it. Not my line of country at all. I just wanted to know if you have ever seen anything of Celia Craddock apart from around Lilac Grove. You know the family and I understand she tried to be rather friendly with you.'

Johnson looked uncomfortable. 'I'm sorry about that kid but not particularly surprised. If ever a girl was out for trouble that one was. I suppose you are sure that sister of hers had nothing to do with it.'

'I'm sure of nothing at the moment but she would have found it difficult to be in two places at once and I can't see any motive.' Henry spoke lightly but managed to give the impression that Janie could still be a suspect.

'Wouldn't be hard to find one where Celia was concerned. Could have been setting her cap at her sister's boy friend.'

'What boy friend?'

169

'The pianist.'

This was interesting. What did Johnson know about Janie's life and how?

'Oh, I didn't realise he was more than her accompanist. How did you know?'

'Word gets around when anyone is as well known as Janie Smith and I heard they were more than friendly.'

'I suppose it's possible.' Henry had no intention of giving this man any information one way or the other.

'Anything could be possible if Janie Smith lost her temper. I knew her when she was a kid and could she let fly! I felt the sting of her hand once. Tall kid for her age. Flew into a rage when I was having a row with another boy. Went for me like a wildcat. Apparently she had a soft spot for the other boy.'

Henry would have liked Janie's version of this, if she remembered. It could be an effort on Johnson's part to throw suspicion on her out of spite but if so he was smiling at the memory. He still hadn't answered Henry's question as to whether he had seen Celia away from Lilac Grove. That could wait for a bit.

'Temper or no temper I hardly think she could have killed her stepfather and then taken his body to Hampstead Heath and dumped it there.' He watched Johnson carefully.

'Good God, when was this?'

'His body was found this morning but he had been dead some time. Not a woman's job, at least, not a woman on her own.'

'No, Craddock was a big man. What would anyone want to kill him for?'

'Your guess is as good as mine.' Henry waited but Johnson had nothing more to say about Craddock. 'You didn't tell me if you have seen anything of Celia away from her home ground. Is is true that she made a pass at you on one or two occasions?'

'It's true all right and I have seen her. Celia didn't take no for an answer and I'm not married. You know how it is?' He shrugged his shoulders.

'Yes, I know,' said Henry, as if he, too, were in the habit of taking on spare females when they made an offer. 'When did she come here? Before she left home or afterwards?'

'Three or four months ago and as far as I know she was living at home.'

'She left home before then. Did you meet her somewhere or had you already given her your address?'

'She just turned up out of the blue.' It was said too quickly and for the first time Henry saw a wary look in Johnson's dark eyes. 'It wouldn't have been difficult for her to get my

171

address. Plenty of people round Lilac Grove know where I live.'

'By the way, where were you last Monday night?'

'I was with a lady friend of mine at Cranbrook Mansions. Two blocks along.'

'Do you mind giving me the lady's full name and address?'

'No; why should I? I don't think it will worry her.' He grinned. 'What on earth do you want to know for?'

'Just routine inquiries. I want to know the whereabouts of anyone who had contact with the girl.'

Johnson looked at him with widening eyes as if suddenly realising the reason for the question. 'Christ! That was the night Celia was killed! So that's why you are here! you thought I might have done it!' He didn't look scared, just shocked.

Henry went down in the lift very thoughtfully. Smooth type, Johnson, but the money-making type often were. Very quick with his alibi for Monday. Was he really so surprised when he remembered it was the night Celia was killed or was that an act? Non-committal about Craddock's murder but if he had a small red car he wasn't the one who picked Craddock up. Better go and see the lady friend now. Mrs. Julia Thornton, 23 Cranbrook Mansions.

Mrs. Thornton was in. A rather flamboyant type with hair bleached to platinum and very long, black lashes. She gave Henry a cool but not unfriendly stare as if weighing up the possibilities. Henry had an insane feeling that she was debating whether to offer her professional services. What she said was, 'Who are you? If you are selling anything I don't want it.'

Henry showed her his card and she raised her eyebrows as if anyone who was anything to do with the police was beneath her contempt.

'I just want to know what you were doing on the evening of the ninth, Mrs. Thornton? That was last Monday.'

'I can't see what on earth it has to do with you.' She looked very indignant and began to bluster. 'Really, these days even when you are in your own home the police won't leave you alone.'

'So you were at home? Alone?'

'No, I wasn't. I don't often spend evenings alone. I like company.'

Damn the woman, she was being awkward on purpose. Why? Just because she disliked the police or because there had been complaints about the gentlemen who called?

'Then I want to know who was with you.'

'As a matter of fact it was a Mr. Johnson who lives along at Brillington Mansions and a Mr. and Mrs. Blayne. What on earth is all this about? She had made no attempt to ask him in. Henry was very definitely de trop.

'Just some routine inquiries. What time did Mr. Johnson come and how long did he stay?'

'He came about eight o'clock but he didn't go until late.'

'How late?'

'I can't see that this has anything to do with you!' Henry stood quite still and waited. 'Oh, well, all right. He didn't go until the morning but that's my business.'

'I'm sure it is.' Henry's smile spoke for itself. 'And Mr. and Mrs. Blayne?' He took out his notebook. 'I just want their address.'

She gave it with an injured air. He couldn't be sure what all the fuss was about. There was no law about having a man to sleep with her, only about keeping a disorderly house. May have been in trouble at some time. Sounded a bit like it. Must check on Mr. and Mrs. Blayne. Someone else could do that. He went back to The Yard.

There was a note on his desk from Halliday. 'I've found a girl who saw Celia Craddock on several occasions last December. Coming back after I've seen Gillian.'

174

Henry began to draw matchmen at a prodigious rate. A big grey car. Who had picked up Craddock? Was it the same car Celia had been seen in? That grey car was driving him bats. Neilson was off the hook for they had already traced the road house where he had had tea and they remembered the man who had paid with a five-pound note. Could the two murders be unconnected? No, he didn't believe that, not after what Craddock had said to Janie. He was bothered, too, about Johnson's remarks about Janie's temper. Why tell him that? Could be because he was a born mischief maker. He drew a matchman with a rock in his hand. Then he got hold of Lloyd and told him to check on the Blaynes. That wouldn't take him long. Halliday came in cock-a-hoop. Gillian was better, much better. He didn't really need to tell Henry. His grin was enough.

'How did you find this girl who saw Celia?'

'Went round all the coffee bars near Neilson's and talked to all the nice little bits of crackling.'

Henry shook his head. 'Boozer, you're downright coarse. And you with a wife!'

Halliday grinned. 'A man can see a girl's attractions even if he is married.' He looked at Henry's matchmen. 'No harm in looking.'

'As long as that's all you do.' Henry smo-

175

thered a grin. Old Boozer and girls! Always liked to give the impression he was a gay dog but in reality he had no eyes for anyone but Gillian.

'What was the girl like?'

'Oh, harmless enough. The sort who likes a bit of fun, that's all. She said she talked to Celia for the sake of someone to talk to while she was waiting for a friend. Later she saw Celia go and sit with two more girls and then the three of them went out together. She said she had seen her with one of the girls a couple of times after that but had never spoken to her again. She was pretty clear in her description of the other two.'

'Not much help unless we can find them.' He drew another little car and then looked up. 'Near Neilson's last December! Where the devil was she living? Is Neilson playing a double bluff? Pick up Craddock and send someone else down to that road house to pay with a five-pound note. It's possible but if he did, my God I'll get him if it's the last thing I do. Blast all this paper work. Lord. I wish I could get this damn case cleared up.' He drew a matchman beside the car. 'If I do there'll only be something else crop up and that won't do.'

Halliday knew what he meant. It would be the bitter end if something else postponed his wedding.

'You could always go sick.'

'And what doctor would give me a certificate? I haven't been sick since I had measles when I was a kid. I'm going to get a meal and not in the canteen. If anyone wants me they can wait.'

When he got back Lloyd was waiting for him with the news that the Blaynes had been with Mrs. Thornton and Johnson until nearly one and that they were a pleasant enough couple. Not flashy. That let Terry Johnson off the hook. Henry drew more cars. They were nagging at him all the time. It was then that he thought of Banstead. A married man who admired Celia. Could he have been friendly with the girl without Janie's knowledge? A possibility. He should have thought of it sooner. He was either getting old or too full of his own affairs. Banstead had remarked how shocked he was too see Janie's display of temper. Funny how it was remarked on. Johnson with amusement, Banstead reluctantly and Craddock with spite.

He picked up the phone and dialled Janie's number. Her rather husky voice came over the line. She gave no number, just asked quickly, 'Who is it?' as if nervous of who it might be.

'Miss Smith, I'm sorry to bother you again

but what sort of car does Mr. Banstead drive?'

'He's got two,' she answered. 'A black Hillman and a dark grey Sunbeam Rapier.'

'Thank you, Miss Smith, goodbye.' He put down the receiver.

'Dear heavens,' he muttered. 'I never gave that man a thought. A dark grey Sunbeam Rapier. Lots of people might mistake it for a Jag if they didn't know a lot about cars. I'm definitely slipping.'

Banstead had admired the girl, thought Janie was jealous and hadn't stinted his words about it. Was that a cover, was he another of Celia's men? It seemed too farfetched but that girl got around and he must make sure. Too late to do anything now but he must put someone on it. No, that was another job he must do himself for it was going to be a delicate business. He was fed up because he was hardly seeing Beth and they should have been on their honeymoon! But it wouldn't be long now. Something to look forward to. The thought was cheering. He looked across at Halliday who was bending over his desk and writing at a furious pace.

'Get along Boozer, it's been a long, long week. I'll get through all these reports in the morning. There may be something I've missed that could give a lead and I won't be coming straight in on Monday. I'm going to see Banstead. I don't suppose there is anything in it but he's got a dark grey car. Not a Jag, a Sunbeam Rapier this time but you can't afford to miss anything. The whole of London seems peopled by those who have enough money to run big, grey cars of one make or another. Before you can look round the coppers will be using them on the beat!'

'Gillian won't be home for two or three weeks, at least I hope she won't. While she is in hospital they'll keep her out of mischief and in the meantime I want to get this backlog up to date. Makes you sick the stuff we have to put on paper, doesn't it? I wonder how much paper work the Bow Street Runners did? I begin to think that any form of education is a mistake! It's just a lot of complicated work that doesn't make any difference to a case one way or the other.'

Henry suddenly grinned. 'Go home and have a hot bath and think of the other side. Bow Street Runners, slops out of the windows and no hot taps to turn on when you feel fed up! No, give me the present day, form-filling and all. I hate bad smells and when I think of London in the old days I feel positively sick.'

'You're fussy!' Halliday grinned back at him but decided a hot bath would be com-

179

forting.

Henry lit a cigarette and muttered his usual, 'I smoke too much!' took his raincoat from the peg and said, 'I wish I didn't keep thinking of cars. Grey cars, anyhow. Celia was seen in a dark grey car. Tom Craddock was murdered within a few hours of being picked up by a man in a grey car. Wherever he was murdered his body was moved afterwards. By the man in the grey car? No, I shouldn't say he was picked up, this was a meeting, a definite meeting, I'm sure. Craddock had come from Hampstead. Probably by Tube to Whitechapel. His own stamping ground but whoever gave him the lift didn't take him home. Where did they go? A disused warehouse where they could talk? Could be anywhere but if the body was put back in the car the bloodstains would be in it unless that battered head was well covered. A rug, sheets of newspaper? Whatever it was it would have to be got rid of. I've a feeling it was something that belonged to the killer or it would have been left with the body, just as the lump of rubble was.'

'What are you going to do? Search the house of everyone who knew Craddock? That's a nice job for someone!'

'Don't be a bigger idiot than you can help. Find someone with a dark grey car who had the opportunity first. What a life. But whoever it was, I'll get him!'

Halliday sighed and Henry glared. There were too many unsolved murders and he knew he was not infallible but two by the same person, and Henry had little doubt of that, usually meant one or two things; the murderer was stupidly cocksure or afraid and in either case that caused mistakes and mistakes were what he relied on—as long as they were not his own!

*   *   *

It rained all day Sunday and on Monday morning the streets were still wet but the sun was shining and it looked like being a beautiful day. Henry was feeling far more cheerful. True, he had spent a great deal of Sunday going through the reports, hunting carefully for any tiny point that would give another lead and finding nothing, but Beth had been there. Pottering about the house, cooking, making endless cups of perfect coffee. A foretaste of what life would be when he and Beth were married.

Banstead was already dictating to a neatly dressed secretary when Henry was shown into his office.

'Get those letters done, Miss Horton, and

I'll give you the others as soon as I am free.'

His quiet manner, his 'Miss Horton' instead of a Christian name, all gave the impression of a correct business man. Nothing free and easy as sometimes happened in anything connected with show business. It could be genuine, it could be a façade. Henry was seldom impressed by externals. He had met too many criminals with perfect fronts to let it cut any ice. On the other hand he often 'felt' a lie. But there were cases in which the wool had been pulled well and truly over his eyes, for a time, at least. Sometimes he thought he was reaching the stage in which he trusted nobody. But he, too, could put up a neat little façade. One which said, without any need of words, 'I haven't the slightest suspicion of you but you know how it is, we have to question everyone!'

'I'm sorry to have to bother you again, Mr. Banstead, but unfortunately we have not yet cleared up these murders. Of course you've seen the account of the father's murder.'

Banstead nodded. 'Yes, a shocking business.'

'It is so difficult to find out anything about the girl before she went to live with her sister. Did she ever approach you about going into show business before then?'

Banstead looked surprised. 'I'd never heard of her existence before she went to live with Janie. I didn't know there was a sister. Actually I knew nothing of Janie's background before this happened. If anyone had asked me I would have said she came from a good, middle-class family. She always had good manners and they were natural. It wasn't until she lost her temper when she heard her sister had been taken up by Neville Neilson that I had a shock.'

'Why?'

'It was as if she dropped the cloak of a gentle disposition and quiet gentility and underneath there was an almost violent character and a slum background.'

'And your impression of her sister?'

'At first a nice, friendly girl who wanted to get into show business but who was overawed by her successful sister and would never do anything to upset her. She didn't speak as well as Janie but these days a slight cockney accent doesn't mean so much as it used to. Children from all parts mix more.' He smiled. 'Take Mary, my youngest, she has developed a north country accent because her dearest friend of the moment comes from Yorkshire. She's twelve. The age when they have great attachments.'

'Unfortunately I haven't any children.

They must be highly entertaining.'

'Too much so at times. Mary is a poppet but wearing. I begin to think I am getting too old to cope with the young. I'm sorry I can't tell you anything more about Celia.'

'You've given me your first impression. What about the second?'

'That she was a liar. She told me she would do what Janie wanted but she must have already seen Neville Neilson. I hope what I've said about Janie's temper won't impress you too much. She's a nice girl and I've always been rather fond of her. Anyone is liable to lose their temper and it must have been infuriating for her sister to go behind her back. I wished afterwards I'd never mentioned it but it slipped out before I gave it a thought. I only hope this trouble won't mess up her life.'

'Why should it?'

He knew well enough but he wanted this man's reactions.

'There's bound to be talk. Show business is broadminded but a nasty piece of publicity can be damaging.'

'And that stepfather of hers didn't do her any good but he can do her no more harm now and no one can hint that she had anything to do with that. Her alibi is absolutely O.K. The last time he was seen alive was getting into a big, grey car on Wednesday afternoon, on the Whitechapel Road.'

Banstead stared at Henry, at first there was astonishment and incredulity and slowly his expression changed to that of sheer amusement.

'So that is the reason for your call and wanting to know if I knew anything of Celia? Somebody has told you I have a big, grey car and you think I could know more about the girl than I have let on. I quite agree I could have done but I didn't and as for the car, on Wednesday it was in for an overhaul and I was driving the Hillman which I usually leave for my wife and it happens to be black. Apart from that I was here until six. On the night the girl was murdered I was at the theatre with a party. The new musical, "Here's to the Girls", and I am interested in one of the girls in the chorus. She's good.'

If Henry had been the blushing sort his face would have been scarlet.

'I'm sorry, Mr. Banstead, but we have to cover every tiny thing and make every inquiry possible. They say you should never speak ill of the dead but that girl was not only a mischief maker but a little slut and I have the job of finding her killer and the killer of her father, not only because nobody wants a murderer free but until he is found there are those who will be convinced that Janie Smith is involved and that girl has been through enough.'

'That's all right. I know how you must feel. Let's hope you get it cleared up as soon as possible. I wish I could give you more help.'

Another dead end! Now where to look? Henry got into his car and sat with his hands on the wheel and stared into space. A big grey car! If he was sure of the make it might be a help but he wasn't. He lit a cigarette and sat smoking thoughtfully. A uniformed officer came towards him, was about to stop and say he shouldn't be there, recognised the Wonder Boy and moved on. Henry saw him out of the tail of his eye. Better move on or he would put the chap in a spot. Probably envying him for being able to drive around in a car instead of treading the beat. Well, he'd done his share of that and he began to think those days were a darn sight easier.

Now he hadn't even a suspect and didn't know where to look for one. Who had that girl been mixed up with during those weeks when she first left home? And why, when she went to her sister, should she be followed and murdered? Not passionate love. The Celias of this world seldom get murdered for that. More and more he was convinced it was to keep her mouth closed. Someone whose position was such that they did not want it known they had associated with her. Someone like Banstead with a loving wife and family who would hate anyone to know they had slipped from grace. Neilson didn't care, Johnson didn't care. What about Max Twyman? Was he as innocent as he seemed! All that talk about her being a cheap little tart. Twyman was hardly top drawer. What he wanted was a little bit of luck and so far he hadn't had any. When he got to The Yard Halliday was grinning from ear to ear.

'I've found one of the girls who was seen with Celia. Young Flossy Bright. I saw her this morning and asked why she'd never been to the police to say she knew Celia. She said she didn't know her, she'd only met her once and the things she said about policemen wasn't at all nice.' The Boozer was obviously tickled pink at the memory. 'If I thought she went to that coffee bar, etcetera, etcetera. She only went there for a bit of company. I said I wasn't interested as to why she went there but what did she know about Celia Craddock and the other girl? The other girl worked in an office and she's never seen her again. Thought she was lonely and glad to talk to someone. Celia said she was going to a party and this other girl went out with her. A very pretty blonde. Not Celia's type at all but if they wanted to go off together it was nothing to do with her.'

'Nothing else?'

'Not much but that little could be just the lead we want. Celia said she was going to get into show business and a chap had set her up in a flat but if he thought she was there to accommodate his friends he'd got another think coming. He was potty if he thought she would make money for him. Flossy told her to be careful. Men who run girls for profit are dangerous but Celia laughed and said she knew what she was doing.'

'Do you think Flossy is scared and that's why she didn't come to us.'

'No, she hasn't a clue who the man is and her attitude is mind your own business and keep out of trouble. She's nobody's fool and I suspect she has a nice little clientele of her own.' Boozer grinned. 'If she knew I think she would have told me. She doesn't see why girls should work to keep a man in luxury!'

'So now we have to look for a pimp! Heaven help us, it could be anyone and certainly not any of the people we have questioned so far. This could be the answer. That fool of a girl getting into the clutches of a man who runs girls for profit. I wonder why he didn't just rough her up or use a razor as an example to others who tried to get out of the game? That's a more common method.'

'Could be more to it than that. Could be that little Celia did some threatening.'

'Could be. You seem to know a nice little line in ladies of easy virtue. Don't you know any of the pimps?'

'There's Johnny the Greek but after he got two years he vowed he'd never have anything to do with women again. Not that he was ever the violent type. Just got shopped for living on immoral earnings. Then there's Blackler but he's still away and likely to be for some time for carving up Susie Manning's face. Donovan is still free but he's taken himself off to Brighton and runs a tobacconists's for cover. I saw Harry Green when he was up here on a case a couple of months ago and he says they'll get Donovan yet.'

'Spare me any more reminiscences. Who do we know and why didn't we think of this possibility sooner? Too convinced it was someone in Janie Smith's circle I suppose.'

'What about Percy the Piper?'

Percy had gained his name because he could play the flute exceedingly well and could have earned a reasonable living by it but Percy wanted more and easier money. He had a nightclub in Soho and his hostesses were always young and pretty. Percy had never been in trouble and on the surface it was very respectable but you never could tell.

'Come along, Boozer, let's go and pay Percy a visit. I don't think for a minute this is anything to do with him but he might be able to point a finger. I'll put the fear of the lord into him if I think he knows anything.'

The club was very exotic and being early in the day it was in the hands of the cleaners but Percy was there. Small and dapper and very elegant. He offered them a drink and minced round the office like a ballet dancer but so daintily that any male dancer would have cringed.

'My dears,' he had the tiniest lips, 'what can I do for you? Anything to help the police. What we would do without you boys I don't know. The roughs and toughs we get around these days! Too dreadful for words. Not that I ever have any trouble. Out patrons move in the nicest circles.'

'I'm sure they do but I'm not interested in your patrons, not just now. I'm much more interested in your girls. Have you ever seen this one?' He brought out an enlargement of one of the pictures of Celia.

'No, she's never been here, I'm sure. Who is she?'

'That's Celia Craddock, the girl who was murdered. Didn't you see her picture in the

190

papers?'

'Yes, but it didn't look like that. You know what newspaper pictures are?' But the small, pinched face had suddenly blanced and Henry was certain it was the name that had shaken him, not the picture. Why? Or was it the thought of murder? It was difficult to tell what would scare anyone like Percy. 'She's not been here, Inspector, never.'

'What do you know about her?'

'Me! I've told you, she's never been here and I've never seen her in my life.'

'I didn't ask if you'd seen her but what do you know about her?'

'How can you know anything about someone you've never seen?' He was doing his best to sound indignant but only sounded scared.

'I expect there are plenty of people you haven't seen but you hear quite a bit about them. Haven't you heard her talked about?'

'My dear, why should I? I don't know anything about her, anything at all,' but try as he would his voice shook.

They were getting warm and Henry knew it but how to shake any information out of this specimen was another thing. He was possibly a crook, even more probbly a 'queer' (which neither interested nor worried Henry), and he was the type who shuddered at violence but he knew something and he was afraid. Who was he afraid of—the police or the criminal?'

'But you know someone who knew her?'

'Of course not. How should I?'

'That's what I'd like to know. How many girls have you here? Hostesses I believe you call them.'

'Twelve, Inspector, all very nice girls.'

'I'm sure they are. I want to see them all.'

'But they are not here now. They don't come until the evening.' He was suddenly on his dignity. 'This is a nightclub and we are open until three in the morning and the girls need their rest.'

'Fine. I'll be back this evening and I want to see them all.'

Henry wished he hadn't said anything for the relief on the little face was plain. As soon as I go, he thought, he'll ring one of those girls and tell her not to come. Oh, well, he could always get the girl's address afterwards. Whoever it was she could hardly vanish into thin air.

'Boozer,' he said as soon as they were in the car, 'I think we are on the trail at last. Which girl knew Celia? I wonder if he'll bribe them all to keep their mouths shut?'

He had intended to spend the evening with Beth but that was off. Never mind, the

192

sooner this case was over the better. He'd have a chat with her on the phone this afternoon.

CHAPTER EIGHT

Henry didn't have a chat with Beth because she wasn't at home and then he remembered Janie's portrait. He was tempted to drop into the house at Hampstead just to catch a glimpse of Beth but couldn't think of an excuse. No, better get on with that paper work and in the meantime it wouldn't be a bad idea to put someone on to keep an eye on Percy's club. No, waste of manpower. Coppers were short enough already and he didn't think there would be anything to gain by it.

'Boozer, any idea who is well in with our Percy? Anyone at all?'

'No, he's the sort to keep well away from tough stuff. Just likes to make a lot of money and I bet he does. Not quite my cup of tea but I've never heard a rumour that he treats his girls badly. Probably takes a percentage of their takings and the fact that they are there encourages a wealthy clientele.'

Halliday decided that Henry was getting much warmer for his matchmen were looking more interesting. They were sitting around at tables with little matchgirls in the shortest skirts and the briefest tops while their hair

194

hung sleekly round their little heads. But Henry's mind was not with them. He was thinking of Beth and wondering what would become of Janie. Would she go back to singing? What about that Roger Phillips? Bad-tempered type. Always gave him the most antagonistic glare.

From Roger Phillips Henry's mind wandered to Neville Neilson and Percy. He surveyed his drawings and thought of all the papers in his intray. He really should do something about them. He sighed deeply, lifted some of them out, put them on top of the matchmen and stared at the top one. Fortunately his phone rang which saved him thinking any more about it. Roger Phillips wanted to know if he could have an interview. He'd got a girl with him who had some information. Henry could hardly believe his ears. Probably quite useless but never turn anyone down.

Roger arrived with a pretty girl in her early twenties.

'This is Lynn O'Farrell who is filling in for Janie at The Purple Pelican. She told me something today which I think could be of use.'

Lynn was looking round the room with surprised eyes. Obviously the sheer utility of it was unexpected. Henry stifled a grin. What did she expect? A James Bond set-up?

'Sit down, Miss O'Farrell, and tell me what you think might be of use.'

'I think I know where Celia Craddock was living before she went to her sister. I only saw her a couple of times and I never thought of it being her until Roger was talking about it today and saying it was a mystery. The first time was when the lift in my block had gone wrong. I ran down the stairs and I saw this girl trying to get into a flat on the next floor. I don't suppose I would have noticed her but she was having difficulty with the key and was pretty mad. I told her to push it right in and then pull it out a little way and it might turn because mine is like that. It worked and I forgot all about it. The next time I saw her she was waiting for the lift. As I got out I asked her if she had had any more trouble with the key, she said she hadn't and that was that.'

'And what makes you so sure it was Celia Craddock now? You didn't think of it when you saw her picture in the papers.'

'Roger said that it wasn't really like her. With different clothes she looked more like her sister and older. Then I remembered that girl. In a way she was like the girl in the picture but she was also like Janie Smith. She was much prettier and, well, tarty, but there

196

was a likeness.' The look she gave Henry was suddenly amused. 'You think I've let my imagination run away with me, don't you, just because Roger talked about her, but I haven't. Look.' Out of her handbag she took one of the pictures of Celia. In heavy pencil she had imposed another hair style and different clothes. 'That's more what she looked like when I saw her and I know it is the same girl.'

The pencilling was clever and the girl so sure.

'When was this?'

'Not long before Christmas because I was rehearsing for a Christmas show.'

Those missing weeks in Celia's life!

'You should be on our staff! An eye for detail. Where do you live, Miss O'Farrell?'

'Pity I didn't think of it sooner. I live in Cranbrook Mansions, Bushgrove Hill.'

Henry wondered if his ears were deceiving him.

'Which floor?'

'The fifth. The girl was going into forty-seven, on the fourth. Between the stairs and the lift.'

And Mrs Thornton, Terry Johnson's friend, lives on the second floor! Curiouser and curiouser. Did Terry Johnson know where Celia was living all the time or was it pure coincidence? Fact was so often stranger than fiction.

'You don't know who is living there now?'

'No idea. The lift has always been working since and you know what it is like in a big block of flats. You might as well be living in the desert. You never know a soul.'

'Thank you very much indeed, Miss O'Farrell. If this girl really was Celia Craddock it may be a great help.'

'It was her all right.' Again that absolute certainty. Almost too sure. Henry was inclined to distrust anything so dogmatic. As if she knew what he was thinking Lynn O'Farrell smiled. 'I was at art school before I started singing. I wasn't much good but I have got an eye for people. The training makes you see clearly.' Her smile grew broader. 'I can't dance to save my life and I'm not much of a singer, either! I'm tempted to join the police.'

'Not much money in it.' Henry was not only amused but he liked the girl.

'Regular though. I'd been out of work for weeks until I took over from Janie and I only just get by.'

'You'd better think it over but we're always looking for recruits. Goodbye, Miss O'Farrell, and thank you.'

Roger had scarcely spoken. His manner to

Henry was of armed neutrality and Henry couldn't think why. When they had gone he turned to Halliday.

'Boozer, take my car and go along to Cranbrook Mansions and see who is living at number forty-seven and ask if they know anything of the girl who was living there between November and February.'

Boozer was back in record time.

'That girl let her imagination run away with her. There's a Mrs. Macdonald living there. She's had the flat for two years but just before Christmas she had her niece staying with her. She was down from Scotland and on her way to Australia to get married. I asked for a description of her and she said she had a photograph. A blonde of about twenty-five with a vague likeness to Miss Smith. A right Charlie I felt. Mrs. Macdonald is a Scot with no two ways about it. A pleasant, middleaged woman with no nonsense and a sense of humour.'

'I'm always wary of people who are so completely sure of anything and yet that girl convinced me she was right by the time she had finished. That's the end of that trail. We still have our Percy's little girls. Nice ones, of course.'

Henry sat and stared thoughtfully at the papers in front of him. He really should do something about it but all the small niggling things irritated when there was something big on. Light broke through.

'Boozer, you'd better try your hand at some of this stuff or you'll never get your promotion. When you've cleared up some of it go and see Gillian. I shan't need you this evening and I must get home and change.'

'You artful old devil! What about your own promotion?'

'It will come, it will come! I may be in a wheelchair by then but who cares!' Henry went, quickly and Halliday grinned. They both knew The Wonder Boy's promotion wouldn't be too long.

Henry rang Beth. 'How's the portrait coming on, darling?'

'Fine but I'm worried about that girl, Henry. Each day she looks a little more lost but not only that, she looks as if she's got something on her mind.'

'Hardly surprising under the circumstances.'

'No, I suppose not and it could be that she is just worried about the future. She says she isn't going back into show business but she doesn't know what she is going to do.'

'Stop worrying about her. Once this is all over she will forget it.'

'I'm not so sure. She is the sensitive type

and things go hard with them. Do you think it will be over soon?'

'Who can say? I hope so. It's got to be before the end of the month. You may have forgotten it, young Beth, but I'm getting married then and they can murder the commissioner for all I care.'

'You sound very determined.'

'I am. Nothing is going to postpone our wedding a second time. I must go, sweet, I've still got a job to do but I love you.'

'Me too, take care of yourself.'

'Never bother to tell a copper that. It's the first thing we learn.'

And the first thing you forget when you are on a job, thought Beth.

Henry was later at the club than he intended. Percy was in a flat spin. His little face looked smaller and thinner than ever and his big, round eyes were as appealing as a frightened fawn, which rather surprised Henry. He suspected Percy was a crook, he didn't think he was a particularly nice type but he looked so anxious, like a mother hen who had lost a chick, clucking all round the place.

'It's Marie-Louise,' he said, looking at Henry as if he were going to cry at any moment. 'She hasn't come and she should have been here over an hour ago.'

'Perhaps she's not well. Give her a ring.'

'That's just it. I have rung and she doesn't answer. If she has gone away somewhere without letting me know I shall be most cross. It's such a naughty thing to do.'

Was Percy really so upset or was this a girl he didn't want Henry to see? Had he rung her up and told her to get out, quickly? It was difficult to know with the Percys of this world. They might be crooks but they were also highly emotional. Time might show but Henry was furious with himself for having been along earlier and given him the opportunity to do anything.

'Has she ever stayed away before?'

'No, but she hasn't been with us long.'

'How long?'

'Just after Christmas.'

'I shouldn't worry. She may turn up later. In the meantime I will talk to the other girls.'

It was a waste of time. He couldn't say one girl was much the same as another for Percy was shrewd and he knew his clientele liked variety but they all said the same thing. They looked at him boldly, coyly, invitingly but not one of them admitted to knowing Celia. There was one thing he would say for Percy—he was certain everyone of them was above the age of consent. Whatever Percy was he managed to keep on the right side of the law and Henry would have bet his bottom dollar that if he took a percentage of the girls' earnings he managed to do it legally, somehow. By the time he had finished with the girls Marie-Louise had still not come and by now he was sure Percy was really worried.

He came into the office in a real flap, insisted on Henry having a whisky and poured himself a coke. He pointed to a cigarette box.

'Do help yourself. I don't smoke or drink. I'm a very nervous person and that would make it worse.'

'I smoke too much.' Percy didn't seem to hear Henry's remark.

'I can't understand it. Felicity says she saw Marie-Louise this afternoon and she didn't say anything about not coming this evening.'

'Then let's have Felicity back.'

Felicity was small and dark with great wide eyes which were made up to look larger than they were. The effect was devastating.

'What time did you see Marie-Louise?'

'I got up at three and had a bath and then I went to Philipe to have my hair done. It was such a mess!' Her great eyes looked at Henry as if appealing to him to say that under no circumstances could she look a mess. Henry did not respond. 'We nearly all go to Philipe. He's marvellous.' Henry wondered how long it would take her to get round to Marie-

Louise. Having discovered that Henry was not in the least interested in her as a proposition she got around to it. 'Marie-Louise was already there.'

'What time was this?'

'About half past four or five. I never do notice time. Marie-Louise was just finished. She said she had been there positively hours being bleached. Her hair was beautiful. Almost silver but just a hint of pink-gold. You've no idea.'

'I'm sure I haven't. What did she say?'

'Just that she'd had her hair done because she thought Sir George . . .' she paused, 'perhaps I had better not tell you his name, after all, but she thought he would be here tonight.'

'So round about five she had every intention of coming.'

'Yes, of course, and I can't think why she hasn't for her friend always comes when she says so.'

Felicity went with a flutter of both eyelashes and skirt.

'Perhaps it would be as well if you gave Marie-Louise another ring.'

Percy dialled a number and listened to the burr-burr with his face in absolutely agony.

'Do you have a key to the girl's flat?'

Percy looked outraged. 'Good gracious,

204

no. The girls have private lives.' Henry wondered how private.

'If you give me her address I'll go round there. I may be able to find out if she has gone away.'

'Would you really? How very kind of you. I'm most perturbed.' His thin hands fluttered and he took a small bottle out of his pocket and opened it. 'This is the only stimulant I indulge in. Smelling salts. So good for my sinuses and they are always giving me trouble. I should really live in the country.' Henry wondered what his boy friend was like for there must be one!

Another flat in another large block. He thought of Lynn's remark, that to live in one was good as living in the desert. You might live in one for years and nobody but the landlord need know you existed. Certainly not your neighbours. He went up in the lift and rang the bell at thirty-three. There was no answer. He tried two or or three times with the same result. Why should the girl have her hair done especially for one man and then not meet him? All his instincts told him there was something wrong. He went down to the foyer. The night porter was browsing in his office.

'Do you know Miss Ambrose who lives in thirty-three?'

The porter grinned. 'She's the pretty one who comes home with the milk. Works in a nightclub.'

'That's right.'

'She won't be in yet.'

'Did you see her go out?'

'No, but she often goes out before I come on and even if she doesn't I don't notice everyone who comes in or out.'

Henry showed him his card. 'She isn't at the nightclub and I am worried and so is her employer. You must have a pass key. Get it and come with me.'

The flat was small but elegant. Wall-to-wall carpeting in the small hall and the living-room door stood open. The same carpeting in the same clear blue. Not a lot of furniture but tasteful. Henry thought he could see Percy's hand. He put his handkerchief over the knob of another door and opened it. There was no need to look farther. Marie-Louise lay on the double bed, fully clothed and apparently asleep. On the bedside table was an empty glass. Henry bent down and smelt it. Whisky. Next to it was a small bottle containing some white tablets. He took the girl's wrist and felt her pulse but there was no need. She was quite cold.

'Go and ring the local police station. Tell them I am here and I've found a dead girl.'

The porter just stood there, horror written all over his face. 'Go along, man, and don't use this phone and don't touch anything as you go out, not even the door-knob.' Not that Henry thought it would make any difference. The only fingerprints they were likely to find was the girl's.

Henry stood and looked down at her. In death she looked very young and innocent. The pale hair with that pink-gold tint was spread out on the pillow and the eyelids were delicately touched with silver-blue. Was it suicide? He didn't think so for one moment and if he had murdered her himself he could not have felt more guilty. What a blundering idiot he had been. Was Percy absolutely innocent? He may not have intended this to happen but he must have rung someone, spoken to someone. There was nothing in the drawers but clothes and he went into the living room. There was a small cocktail cabinet but it did not contain much. An open bottle of whisky. All the other bottles were sealed.

A reproduction Queen Anne bureau held a few letters and photographs. Clearly her family. Loving letters from her mother written on cheap paper, telling her to take care of herself and not to work too hard. They were delighted she had such a good job.

Thanked her for the money which was such a blessing with her father ill but she mustn't go short for them. They hoped she would be able to come and see them soon. The address was in Durham. Poor devils, they thought she was working as a secretary. He didn't envy the person who had to break the news to them.

The local police came with the doctor and all the usual paraphernalia. Henry told them all he knew and left. Back to Percy. He was fluttering in his office.

'Did Marie-Louise's friend put in an appearance?'

'Yes and he was rather upset because she wasn't here.'

'Did you give him any reason for her not being here?'

'I didn't need to. He asked me to tell her he had gone straight home. He didn't stay long.'

'What time did he come?'

'It was after eleven.'

'I want his name and address.'

'Whatever for? We don't give the names of our clients. They don't always . . .' Percy stopped dead and looked pleadingly at Henry.

'I know they don't want their wives to know where they have their after-office business meetings but this is a case when I have to

208

have it. Marie-Louise is dead.'

If he had hit poor Percy over the head the reaction couldn't have been greater. He slumped down in the nearest chair and his face went as white as paper.

'Now you had better tell me everything you know.'

'But I don't know anything! I'm most terribly shocked. She was such a nice girl.' The little lisp was even more pronounced and Henry realised it was not affectation at all. He tried to control it but in moments of stress he couldn't. His small hands were shaking like butterflies on a flower.

'You mean she was a nice girl until she came to work?' Henry was brutal on occasions. 'How many nice girls have become whores in this place and who had their dirty hands on her before she came here?'

'I don't know what you are talking about. Felicity brought her here. She had been working in an office and not making much money.'

'If Felicity hasn't gone home with one of her gentlemen friends I want to see her.'

Felicity came. A very frightened Felicity.

'Why didn't you tell me you knew Marie-Louise before she came here to work?'

'You didn't ask me and I never thought about it. I didn't know her. I just met her at a party in Chelsea. She was very pretty and very fed up because London wasn't what she expected and she wasn't making enough money to live on decently. I said Percy might take her on and she would make money dancing with the gentlemen than she could make as a secretary.'

'Just dancing?' Henry looked straight into the girl's big eyes. She tossed her head.

'Because we work here we don't have to sleep around!' Felicity was indignant. 'Marie-Louise never complained about anything here. She seemed to be having a good time.'

'She didn't talk about her family?'

'No.'

No, thought Henry, thinking of that pathetic letter.

'Can you remember anyone else who was at that party?'

'No. It was Christmas Day and I had to get here in the evening. It was an awful crowd. Marie-Louise, she was Mary, then, looked miserable and I talked to her. She was with another girl. Not her sort at all.' She stopped and her eyes opened wide with something close to horror in them. 'Oh, God, let me see that girl's picture again.' She looked at the picture of Celia. 'I don't know. It could have been her but I only saw her once. Marie-Louise said she only met her a few days before in a coffee bar. It was one of those queer parties in which people were coming and going all the time.'

'Who gave it?'

'An artist I knew slightly. It was a farewell thing because he was off to Paris in the new year. I don't know anything else, honestly.'

'All right, it doesn't matter. I shan't want you any more and I shouldn't tell anyone about this.'

The girl who worked in an office and had been picked up by Celia Craddock in a coffee bar. If she hadn't been lonely she would still be alive. If he hadn't come here this afternoon she might be. Henry hated himself. Had Celia merely been friendly or was she trying to procure little Mary Ambrose? That was something they would never know. Percy was adamant that he had told no one that Henry had been there in the afternoon.

'Really, Inspector, I wouldn't want to publicise the fact that you were here!'

He didn't know the address of Marie-Louise's friend, just his name. Henry didn't need his address. He knew his office but that would have to wait until the morning. When he left The Little Fawn, the sun was shining.

After three hours sleep he was refreshed. Thank goodness he had not lost the capacity for instant sleep. His mind was still on cars.

It was if they were haunting him. Sir George was a very eminent business man and the director of a number of companies. His office was in a new block in the city. Nothing to do with show business, thought Henry, with great satisfaction.

Henry's card was an open sesame. Sir George was heavily built, a middle-aged man with a quiet, well-bred efficiency oozing from every pore. Henry wondered if he had told his wife where he was going last night.

'What can I do for you, Inspector Mason? It can't be a parking offence or they wouldn't send you. Not that my car is ever left where it would be in the way. We have an underground garage.'

'What make of car?'

Sir George looked puzzled. 'A grey Bentley. Then it is something to do with the car.'

Another damn grey car!

'Not exactly, sir, but I am interested in cars just now. Do you mind telling me where you were yesterday between five p.m. and eleven. I know where you were after that. The Little Fawn, although you didn't stay long.'

Sir George didn't even look uncomfortable.

'I was here with my secretary until six-thirty. Then I bathed and changed. I have a small suite here, it saves so much time. I had to be quick for I was dining with friends of mine at seven-thirty and they live at Princes Gate. Mr. and Mrs. Hugh Stapleton.' He smiled. 'I gather you wanted their names. I stayed with them until getting on for eleven.'

'I take it you will not mind your secretary confirming the time you finished work?'

'Of course I don't. You wouldn't ask unless there was a good reason.'

He pressed a bell and a very correct young man came in. A male secretary!

'Marshall, what time did you leave last night?'

'It was nearly seven, sir. You went to have your bath at six-thirty. Is there something wrong?'

'No, Marshall, I just want to confirm the time.'

The secretary went as quietly as he had come.

'Now if I ring Mr. Stapleton you can ask him any questions you wish.'

It was all done very smoothly and Sir George did not appear to mind in the slightest.

'Now do you mind telling me what all this is about? You wouldn't want to know all this for fun.'

'You were friendly with a girl called Marie-

Louise at The Little Fawn?'

'Yes.' He made no attempt to beat about the bush and he didn't seem to notice the past tense. 'She's rather a sweet girl. Not the usual type. There isn't any point in my denying it for obviously you know but what it has to do with you I can't think. I stay in town two nights a week as a rule. We have a house at Brighton and my wife is a complete invalid. Even if she knew about Marie-Louise I doubt if it would hurt her, poor soul. She has a nurse with her all the time. She had a severe stroke four years ago and she is more dead than alive. Now will you tell me why you are here?'

'I found Marie-Louise dead in her flat last night. An overdose of something but I don't know yet what it was.'

'Dear God!' There was no doubt of the shock on Sir George's heavy features. 'Why should she do that? As far as I know it was nothing to do with her relationship with me. She knew just how I felt about her. Fondness and gratitude for making my life a little brighter. Financially I was looking after her and I wanted her to give up her work. Believe me, she was not the promiscuous type and I know she was helping her family. What could have made her do such a thing?'

'I don't think she did do it, Sir George. I

214

believe she was murdered.'

'So that is why you wanted to know where I was. Inspector Mason, I wouldn't have harmed her for anything on earth. If you had met her you would know why. I'll tell you something else. I was the first man that girl had given herself to and when I realised it I was ashamed. Who on earth could have done such a thing and why?'

'That's what I want to know. I don't think you need worry about your name being mentioned in this. When did you see her last?'

'On Friday. Last night I didn't intend to stay, anyhow. My wife wasn't so well when I left in the morning and I went home. I'd like to do something for the girl's family. I suppose they'll have to know where she was working.'

'Yes, I'm afraid so but they need not know too much. If you do give help be careful how you do it. Thank you for being so co-operative. It makes our work easier.'

But not much, he thought, as he drove towards The Yard. He couldn't help feeling pity for Sir George, the man was genuinely cut-up but he was as far away from a solution as ever. Put out an appeal for anyone who had seen Celia during those weeks. Somebody must have done. He wished Lyn O'Farrell had been right about seeing her but it was amazing how so many girls looked alike these days. Three murders and he was sure they were all connected in some way. What did that fluttering 'queer' Percy know. The trouble with his type was that although they panicked they still hung on to knowing nothing. You could question and question but it would still be, 'Really, Inspector, I don't know a thing!' Percy would have to look out for he was going to put a tail on him now and set inquires afoot. Pity he hadn't done it before. It was too strange altogether that as soon as he began asking him questions one of his girls was killed and the very one that had been with Celia and he had no doubt in his mind that Felicity was right.

A few hours later he had the shock of his life. Percy was married and had two children. His wife was a nice, homely body and they had a flat near Hyde Park! What was more he had nothing to do whatever with where his girls have lived. But it wasn't until later they discovered he had been brought up not far from Lilac Grove. He had left there in his teens and for a time played sax in a dance band but it wasn't much of a band. It had fallen by the wayside. Then he started a snack bar in a sleazy district and made money out of it and started another one. He sold them both and opened his nightclub. The girls were the attraction and the men who frequented it had money. Apart from his expensive flat he lived quietly and they didn't even keep a maid!

But Lilac Grove! He swore he had never seen Celia but was it the truth? He was a different age group and he hadn't been seen in the district for years. Probably wanted to forget he had ever been there. But it was a connection. Somebody he knew knew Celia and Celia knew Marie-Louse. What about a car? Lloyd grinned.

'One of his extravangances. A whopping big American job but he doesn't drive. Scared sick of anything mechanical. Sometimes his wife drives him but more often than not a man called Thomas. An odd-job man and he actually likes Percy. Says he's a good boss and a doting husband and father.'

'Oh, dear, how taken in can you be? Probably the worst he does is to get the right girls for his club, charge the earth for meals and drinks and fiddle his income tax. I've enough to do without worrying about that. It's this connection with Lilac Grove that gets me. I suppose he doesn't own any property there?'

'The only freehold property he seems to have is a little cottage by the sea where his wife takes the kids for the summer and he goes down as often as he can.'

Henry was browned off and rang Beth but doubted whether she would be back at her friend's yet but she was.

'Janie told me she had someone coming to see her so I left early. I hope it was that Roger Phillips because I think she is fond of him. I wonder if he's let her down and that's why she seems worried. Perhaps he got scared of the publicity.'

'Didn't give me that impression. I thought he was trying to protect her from me. Thought I was a snooping brute who wouldn't leave the poor girl alone.'

'Henry, you are funny but I do wish this business was over. Janie is beginning to look downright ill.'

'I'm doing my best.' Henry was slightly annoyed. Anyone would think he didn't want it cleared up!

'Of course you are, darling, I know that. But I really am worried. I believe Janie thinks she knows something. This afternoon she said she didn't think Celia left Lilac Grove at all.'

'Did she though! I think I had better go and see her again.'

'I wish you would. Somehow I think she may have more of the answer than she knows.'

'O.K. darling. Don't worry your little

head.'

He looked up to see Halliday standing just inside the door with a wide grin on his face. 'Take that grin off your face. Lilac Grove, Boozer! What have we missed? I wonder if Terry Johnson can put us on to someone who has made money. Let's look him up again.'

The flats had a wing at either end and a drive-in that made parking easy. A red Anglia stood by the kerb. Cars, cars! And then it clicked over. Terry Johnson had a red Anglia but it had been smashed up. It was instinct that led him straight to the porter.

'Whose red Anglia is that outside?'

'Mr. Johnson's sir. He often leaves it there and it isn't in the way so I don't bother.'

'I thought he'd had a bad smash. Don't tell me this is a new one.'

'Oh, no, sir. It was his Jag he smashed.'

'Really. I didn't know he had two cars. What colour was his Jag?'

'Dark grey. A lovely job.'

'I'm going up to see him.'

'He's not in, sir. He went out about an hour ago but I don't suppose he has gone far or he would have taken his car?'

'That's all right, I can give him a ring or call some other time.'

As Henry and Halliday got back in the car Henry muttered, 'My God, I must be slipping. Why did I never think about him having another car?'

'What about his alibi?'

'What about it? We are going to pay the Blaynes a visit and I only hope they are in.'

Both Mr. and Mrs. Blayne were home. Pleasant, ordinary and not terribly intelligent. Yes, of course they were right when they said they were at Mrs. Thornton's until getting on for one, well, after midnight, anyhow.

'And Mr. Johnson was with you all the time?'

'He was there all the time.' Mrs. Blaynes looked uncomfortable. 'As a matter of fact, Inspector, it was rather embarrassing. He said he had a rotten headache and was going to bed. It wasn't much after nine. You see he only lives a little way away and Mrs. Thornton had only one bedroom and we could hear him moving about in it. It was so obvious. It wasn't our business but I thought it such bad taste.'

'What happened then?'

'We suggested going home and Mrs. Thornton persuaded us to stay and play cards but really we would much rather have come home.'

'You didn't see any more of Mr. Johnson?'

'No, after about ten minutes it was so quiet

so I suppose he had gone to sleep and when we left the bedroom door was shut.'

'So he might not have been there at all?'

She looked startled. 'I suppose not. I never thought about it.'

Mr. Blayne looked annoyed. 'But why should any man give the impression he was spending the night with a woman when he was going home?'

'Perhaps because he wasn't going home, Mr. Blayne. I gather you are not close friends?'

Mr. Blayne shook his head. 'We only met them casually over a drink and we've never been there since.'

'I think you have been made use of. A nice, respectable couple who would tell the truth. Are you prepared to say you never saw Mr. Johnson after nine-thirty at the latest on that night? In court if necessary?'

'Yes, if necessary. I don't like being used.'

'Thank you and please don't mention this to anyone.'

'Bang goes Terry Johnson's alibi for the night Celia was killed but he will keep. He's convinced we are off the mark. Let's go and see if Janie Smith does know something or thinks she does.'

They reached her house at twilight but there was no lights on. Henry rang the bell but there was no answer. Where was Fanny? Henry felt the hairs on the back of his head tingling. There was something wrong, he was sure of it. The worst of this house was the windows were too high from the ground to see in.

'Damn these old houses with semi-basements! They're a blasted nuisance. Well, I'm getting in, Boozer. I've got a nasty feeling in my bones.'

They managed to get in at the kitchen window. Instinctively Henry made for the lounge. She was lying back in an armchair breathing heavily. In front of her was a tray with tea things. Her teacup was almost empty.

'Ring for an ambulance, Boozer, and look sharp. She's in a bad way. Tell them to move like the devil or we'll have another death on our hands.'

This time there was no bottle, just a little white cardboard box with no identity as to where it came from but inside were two neatly folded paper packets. He opened one, touched the white powder with his finger and tasted it. Very little taste at all but he went to the kitchen sink and washed his mouth. The ambulance was there in record time and Henry breathed a sigh of relief to know there was a hospital not far away.

'I'll go with her, Boozer. You wait for the housekeeper and tell her what has happened.'

Henry hung about the sister's office. Then he remembered Roger Phillips. Try The Purple Pelican first. He had just arrived. Henry asked him to come to the Hampstead Hospital immediately. It didn't take him long and although his suit was impeccable his hair was awry.

'What on earth has happened? It's Janie, isn't it?'

'Yes, an overdose of some drug or other.'

'But she never takes drugs. She won't even take an aspirin unless the doctor says so.'

'I don't think she took this on her own accord. Did you know if she was expecting a visitor today?'

'No, I haven't seen her for a couple of days. We—we had a bit of a row.'

'I thought you might have done. Beth was worried about her.'

'Who on earth is Beth?'

'The woman who is painting her portrait. She happens to be my fiancée.'

'And you had the nerve to put her on to spy?'

'No, it was nothing to do with me. Beth wanted to paint her portrait and when Beth wants to do a thing she usually does it. She likes Janie Smith and told me she was worried. So I went along, thank goodness.'

Roger cooled down and a doctor came into the office.

'She's going to be all right. You caught her in time.'

'Can I see her?' Roger almost shouted.

'No you can't, whoever you are, and she won't be in a condition to speak to you until the morning, Inspector.'

'I'll wait.' Roger sat down as if that settled it.

Henry gave a sudden smile. 'Is there any reason why he shouldn't. I'm sure he'll do exactly as he is told and it might be good for her to see someone she knows when she is conscious. And this is not attempted suicide but attempted murder. I'll be sending one of my men along but she's not in any danger now.'

'If you hadn't gone to see her she would have died.' It was the first time Roger had given Henry anything but a glare.

'It's possible.'

'More than that,' said the doctor. 'We only just managed to save her and she's going to need careful nursing.'

Roger put out his hand. 'Thank you, Inspector Mason. Sorry if I've been a bit of a swine but I've been terribly concerned over Janie.'

'I know and I've felt pretty bad about it myself but when you can say anything tell her she has nothing to worry about. We'll have the man in custody in a very short time now. Before she wakes up in fact.'

When he got back to the house Fanny was weeping copiously and Halliday was making tea.

'Don't worry, Fanny, she's going to be all right.' Henry put a hand on her shoulder. 'Mr. Phillips is at the hospital and you can go there first thing in the morning.'

Henry and Halliday went back to The Little Fawn. It was a beautiful name. It suited Percy perfectly and now his eyes were so big and his face so pinched Henry knew he had a lot of things on his mind.

'It isn't any use beating about the bush, Percy. Who did you ring up after I made inquiries about Celia Craddock? You told somebody and because of it Marie-Louise was killed.'

'I never rang anyone, Inspector, honestly.' Percy collapsed limply on the nearest chair.

'You let Terry Johnson know I had been here, didn't you?'

'Terry Johnson! No, I didn't need to.' Percy straightened up and looked almost dignified. 'He was here when you came. He saw your car and was quite rude and said he would wait in the kitchen until you had gone.'

'And then he came and asked you what I wanted?'

'No, he guessed.'

'Have you been seeing a lot of him lately?'

Percy went very white. 'More than I want.'

'Protection or drugs?'

'It isn't much use denying it, is it?' Percy was no longer fluttering. From somewhere in that small body he had summoned up an unexpected courage but there was black despair in his dark eyes. 'Protection to start with and now it's drugs, too.' He was speaking slowly, fighting to control that lisp. 'I won't deal in drugs. My kid sister—she's in a home.'

'Why didn't you go to the police?'

'With no proof!' Percy clenched his small fists. 'Don't tell me you'd give me protection. Have you enough men? I've a wife and children.'

'Did you know he killed Celia Craddock?'

'No, he said he had been with friends on the evening she was killed but I knew he had set her up in a flat and he told me to keep my mouth shut.'

'And you were too scared to say anything.'

'Yes, Inspector, much too scared but I

didn't know a girl would be killed because of it. I didn't know any of the girls knew Celia Craddock but I knew Craddock and Johnson were sometimes mixed up together.'

'You've been an awful fool, Percy, but we've broken Johnson's alibi. Do you know where he had Celia parked during those weeks?'

'Yes, in Cranbrook Mansions.'

Halliday let out a quiet, 'Blimey!'

'The nice Scotswoman,' muttered Henry. So Lynn O'Farrell had seen Celia.

Terry Johnson went quietly but said it was an outrage and he didn't intend to say anything until he saw his solicitor. Mrs. Thornton and Mrs. Macdonald were even more outraged but Henry knew they wouldn't save Johnson's skin at the expense of their own.

CHAPTER NINE

It was a couple of days before Henry was able to have a conversation with Janie Smith. She was lying with her hand held fast in Roger's and he murmured, 'She's doing fine.' Henry could see that. The lost look had gone completely. It was as if she had at last found a home.

'I'll come back later,' he said. 'It's not important. We've got Johnson safe under lock and key.'

'No, don't go, I want to tell you just what happened and I'm feeling fine now.'

Henry sat down and Janie held on to Roger's hand.

'After you talked about Terry Johnson I couldn't get him out of my mind. There was something that kept nagging me and I couldn't remember what. Then, while Beth was painting, she said something about people putting up a barrier so that you don't really see them. My mind was wandering but I thought how right she was. A barrier! Barry! That was it. Out of the blue.'

Henry stared at her. 'I don't get it. What do you mean?'

'I told you how I found that boy Draper at

home once. The next day I tried to get through to Fanny but the line was engaged every time. When I did get through Fanny said Celia had been talking to that Terry for goodness knows how long. You see I took it for granted it was the boy I had seen but I suddenly remembered that you had said his name was Barry. Then who was Terry? Could it be Terry Johnson? If so, did he know anything about Celia? Fanny was going to see her sister so I thought it was a good chance to talk to him. I looked up his number and rang him up.'

'Were you suspicious of him?'

'No, I just wanted to find out if he knew anything but I think he thought I was. I rather pushed Beth out but I thought he wouldn't talk if anyone else was there.'

'How right you were and Beth thought you were expecting Roger.'

'No, did she really. I'd just made myself a cup of tea when Terry came. The milk was already in the cup. As soon as I opened the door I wished I hadn't asked him.'

'Were you afraid?'

'No, I just loathe his type. Slick and smooth-tongued. Knowing all the answers. Perhaps they remind me too much of Lilac Grove. Not that I think it will ever worry me again.'

Henry looked at the secure way Roger was holding her hand and thought she was right.

'I asked him in and told him I wanted to know where Celia had been before she came to me because I was sure he had been seeing her. I thought he would deny it but he just grinned and said that was his business. I said it was mine, too. He gave me an odd look and then I remembered something. I saw him as a boy again and he had a big stone in his hand and was just going to hit another boy with it when someone stopped him. In that moment I was sure he had killed Tom Craddock. My stepfather knew something and had tried to get money out of Terry as he had out of me. I didn't stop to think. I just said. "You killed Tom Craddock because he knew you killed Celia!" Terry burst out laughing and said I was out of my mind.'

'I said I was going to phone the police and he let me go. I began to feel silly. He wouldn't let me phone the police if he had really killed them! As I picked up the phone he called out, 'Don't be an idiot, of course I didn't kill them. You don't think the police haven't been making inquiries. They know just where I was at the time. But I do have my own suspicions. Let's have a cup of tea and I'll tell you what I've found out and then we can call the police.' He sounded so reasonable and I wondered if I had let my imagination run away with me. I went and fetched another cup and saucer, poured out the tea and drank it. It tasted rather bitter but I thought that was because it had been standing too long. Terry drank his and began to tell me something about Tom Craddock but I couldn't understand because I was sleepy. The next thing I knew I was here and Roger was holding my hand.'

'You're a very lucky young woman. That man is a cold-blooded killer but, like many before him, he was too clever, had too many irons in the fire and thought the police too stupid.'

'But why did he kill Celia?'

'I think she knew enough about Johnson to put him behind bars for a long, long time and she was probably blackmailing him.'

'Why did she come to me at all?'

'She may have really wanted to get into show business and thought she could do it the easy way. Plenty of people are convinced it doesn't mean hard work. When you wouldn't help and Neilson was getting fed up she may have stepped up her demands to Johnson, who knows? Greed can make people very stupid.'

'I suppose so. Do you think Beth would come and see me soon?'

'She'd be delighted.'

Roger was still holding her hand when Henry left.

*　　*　　*

Beth and Henry were sitting on a bench in the park, watching the sun set in a red splendour.

'Do you think your brother can possibly get here safe and sound in time for the wedding? For I warn you, young Beth, it is not going to be postponed again!'

'I had a letter this morning saying he is making wonderful progress and will be here in plenty of time. His leg will still be in plaster but he is determined to see you make an honest woman of me!'

'What a nice type!'

'He is, darling, you'll like each other. I'm going to do another portrait of Janie Smith when we come back from our honeymoon. I know the other one isn't finished but at least I caught her expression. Now I'm going to do one as she looks now.'

'I believe in fairy stories.' Henry was holding Beth's hand and didn't care if the copper coming towards them recognised him. 'On the other hand I never thought I would meet the Sleeping Beauty.'

'I know just how you feel. Do you think Roger did wake her with a kiss and she suddenly discovered that being loved wasn't revolting after all?'

'Highly probable but don't go to sleep here just to see how it feels. I should just walk off and leave you.'

'Henry Mason, you wouldn't dare!'

'No,' said Henry, well content, 'I wouldn't dare!'

Union Free Library
North Providence, R. I.

To take a book from the Library
without having it charged is an offense
against the rights of other readers, and
a violation of the rules of the Library
and the laws of the State.

Examine this book carefully before
taking it home. If found to be dam-
aged or needing repairs, report it.
Otherwise, you will be held respon-
sible for its condition.

OCT 1 2 1982